"A terrific collection of stories—fiercely and beautiful made."

—Joy Williams

"In the eleven stories of *Sabrina & Corina*, Fajardo-Anstine writes a love letter to the Chicanas of her homeland—women as unbreakable as the mountains that run through Colorado and as resilient as the arid deserts that surround it. . . . In her fierce, bold stories, these women—and she—are seen, and heard, and made known; the collection is both a product of pain and a celebration of survival. . . . Like the woman on *Sabrina & Corina*'s cover, the hearts of these characters are exposed but intact. Fajardo-Anstine's heart is there on the page, too, beating with the blood of her ancestors."

—*Bustle*

"Eleven achingly realistic stories set in Denver and southern Colorado bear witness to the lives of Latina women of Indigenous descent trying to survive generations of poverty, racism, addiction, and violence. . . . Fajardo-Anstine writes with a keen understanding of the power of love even when it's shot through with imperfections. . . . Fajardo-Anstine takes aim at our country's social injustices and ills without succumbing to pessimism. The result is a nearly perfect collection of stories that is emotionally wrenching but never without glimmers of resistance and hope."

—*Kirkus Reviews* (starred review)

"Latina and Indigenous American women who long to be seen—and see themselves—are the beating heart of the stories in Fajardo-Anstine's rich and radiant debut. . . . Sharing her characters' southern Colorado homelands, Fajardo-Anstine imbues her stories with a strong sense of place and the infinite unseen generations that coexist in even single moments."

—*Booklist* (starred review)

"In Fajardo-Anstine's beautiful debut collection, set largely in Denver, Colorado, she dexterously explores what it means to be Latina, indigenous, and female in ways both touching and powerful. . . . These stories are stirring meditations on the lives of Latinas of indigenous ancestry; Fajardo-Anstine's collection is vividly alive with the love and pain of its characters, while echoing with the spiritual power of their pasts."

—*Publishers Weekly*

"Fajardo-Anstine's debut short-story collection shines a light on indigenous Latinas living in the Southwest. *Sabrina & Corina* is a provocative glimpse into the violations of culture, homelands and women's bodies. In 'Sugar Babies,' a daughter is tasked at school to take care of a baby made out of a sugar sack, tending to it as her estranged mother could not do for her. In 'Julian Plaza,' two young sisters spend time at a housing facility for the elderly while their dying mother suffers from their inability to pay for better cancer treatments."

—*Ms. Magazine*

"Kali Fajardo-Anstine writes about hard truths in women's lives so knowingly, and with such a deft touch, I felt hyperalert, as well as implicated and imperiled. The book is about belief, coping, yearning, and proceeding in spite of adversity (that is, the times we stay alive). The final act of the first story tells us everything we need to know about what territory we'll be entering: In these achingly convincing stories, the writer is writing delicately, symbolically, about mortality itself."

—ANN BEATTIE

"Like the best debut short story collections, *Sabrina & Corina* reveals a literary voice that simply hasn't been heard before. See a world that's never before been caught on the page. Watch how it dances with a straight razor. Realize you've been cut when it's already too late."

—MAT JOHNSON, author of *Loving Day*

"I haven't had time to read many collections this year, but I've found time to read and re-read *Sabrina & Corina,* by Kali Fajardo-Anstine. It is a beautiful, masterfully written collection of multi-generational stories featuring Chicana characters in Colorado, and each story reads like the best chapter of a novel—I love when I can say that about a work of art that is so commit-ted to the humanity, culture, and familial love of a people to whom dominant narratives have often spoken over. Read this book."

—*Kenyon Review*

"[A] beautiful collection."

—*HelloGiggles*

"[An] engrossing collection of tales . . . stories that bravely re-invent the Wild West narrative by lifting up Latinx women and portraying callused-hand cowboys not as heroes, but as villains and perpetrators of violence."

—*Latino Book Review*

"You will clutch your heart reading Kali Fajardo-Anstine's short story collection. . . . Her stories are that heartbreaking, each one like a gift from a small child, offered with earnest, luminous eyes, innocence itself, impossible to reject. . . . Go find yourself a copy of this thrilling, touching, beautiful book."

—*New York Journal of Books*

"In [*Sabrina & Corina*] we find a different narrative of the West. These are women who inhabit a space between the Indigenous and the Latinx; they are fierce [and] powerful in their own way."

—*The Brooklyn Rail*

"Each story showcases Fajardo-Anstine's mastery of prose and the vulnerability of her characters. A timely classic in the making, *Sabrina & Corina* is a crucial read."

—*Read It Forward*

"A powerful, passionate collection of stories centered on the experience of Latina women in the Southwest . . . Fajardo-Anstine's voice is fresh and unstinting, her vision complex and bold. *Sabrina & Corina* is an important, delightful, dazzling debut."

—ALYSON HAGY, author of *Scribe*

# SABRINA

# &

# CORINA

# SABRINA
# & CORINA

*Stories*

## Kali Fajardo-Anstine

ONE WORLD
NEW YORK

Published in the United States by One World, an imprint of Random
House, a division of Penguin Random House LLC, New York.

ONE WORLD and colophon are registered trademarks
of Penguin Random House LLC.

Originally published in hardcover in the United States by One World,
an imprint of Random House, a division of Penguin
Random House LLC, in 2019.

Stories from this collection have appeared in the following publications:
"Any Further West" in the Boston Review; "Remedies" in the *Bellevue
Literary Review*; "Sisters" in *Heck Magazine*; "All Her Names" in the
*American Scholar*; "Sugar Babies" in *Southwestern American
Literature*; "Sabrina & Corina" in the *Idaho Review*.

Grateful acknowledgment is made to Dwarf Music for permission
to reprint an excerpt from "Sad-Eyed Lady of the Lowlands" by Bob
Dylan, Copyright © 1966 and copyright renewed 1994 by Dwarf Music.
All rights reserved. International copyright secured.
Reprinted by permission.

LIBRARY OF CONGRESS CATALOGING-IN-PUBLICATION DATA
Names: Fajardo-Anstine, Kali, author.
Title: Sabrina & Corina : stories / by Kali Fajardo-Anstine.
Description: First edition. | New York : One World, [2018]
Identifiers: LCCN 2018023965 | ISBN 9780525511304 (paperback) |
ISBN 9780525511311 (ebook)
Classification: LCC PS3606.A396 A6 2018 | DDC 813/.6—dc23
LC record available at https://lccn.loc.gov/2018023965

Printed in the United States of America on acid-free paper

oneworldlit.com
randomhousebooks.com

6 8 9 7

Book design by Caroline Cunningham
Title page image: iStock.com/SeanXu

*For my mama and papa,*

*creators of artists*

*With your childhood flames on your midnight rug*

*And your Spanish manners and your mother's drugs*

*And your cowboy mouth and your curfew plugs*

*Who among them do you think could resist you?*

*Sad-eyed lady of the lowlands*

—BOB DYLAN

# CONTENTS

. . . . . . . . . . . . . . . .

# SABRINA
# &
# CORINA

# SUGAR BABIES

. . . . . . . . . . . . . . . . .

Though the southern Colorado soil was normally hard and cakey, it had snowed and then rained an unusual amount that spring. Some of the boys in my eighth-grade class decided it was the perfect ground for playing army. They borrowed shovels and picks from their fathers' sheds, placing the tools on their bicycle handlebars and riding out to the western edge of our town, Saguarita, a place where the land with its silken fibers of swaying grass resembled a sleeping woman with her face pressed firmly to the pillow, a golden blonde by day, a raven-haired beauty by night.

The first boy to hit bone was Robbie Martinez. He did so with the blunt edge of a rusted shovel. Out of the recently drenched earth, he lifted a piece of brittle faded whiteness and tossed it downwind like nothing more than a scrap of paper. "Look," he said, kneeling as if he was praying. "Everybody come look."

. . . . . . . .

The other boys gathered around. There in the ground lay broken pieces of bowls with black zigzagging designs. Next to those broken bowls were human teeth, scattered like dried kernels of yellow corn. Above them the sun had begun to fade behind the tallest peak of the Sangre de Cristo Mountains. The sky was pale and bleak, like the bloated belly of a lizard passing above.

"Don't touch it," Robbie said. "None of it. We need to tell somebody."

And tell they did. The entire town. Everyone, it seemed, was a witness.

Days after their discovery, our final eighth-grade project was announced. We gathered in the gym for an assembly. The teachers brought together the boys from technical education class and the girls from home economics. We sat Indian style in ten rows beneath dangling ropes and resting basketball hoops. The room smelled like a tennis ball dipped in old socks and the cement walls were padded in purple vinyl—supposedly to minimize dodgeball injuries. I thought it looked like a loony bin.

Mrs. Sharply, a bug-eyed woman with a neck like a giraffe's but a torso like a rhino's, stood before us on a wooden box. "For the remaining two weeks of your junior high career," she said, "you will care for another life." She then reached behind her into a paper grocery bag, revealing a sack of C & H pure cane sugar. "Sugar babies. We will be raising our very own sugar babies."

Older kids had gossiped about notorious school projects. We had heard stories of piglet dissections, the infamous "growing and changing" unit, rocket launches with carbon dioxide canisters, and a cow's lung blackened and doused in cigarette smoke, but no one had warned us about this.

"Sugar babies are a lot of responsibility," Mrs. Sharply said as she stepped down from her box and paced with the sugar sack. She explained we were to be graded on skills like feeding, bonding, budgeting, and more. She then passed around diaper directions.

"We do it all alone?" It was Solana Segura. She was behind me, her perpetual whimper causing every sentence to end like a little howl. "Like single moms and stuff?"

Somewhere, down the rows, a boy croaked, "But the DNA shows I am *not* the father."

We chirped with laughter until Mrs. Sharply held up two fingers, signaling silence. "Of course not. You'll be in committed partnerships. We're drawing names."

A teacher's aide in Payless flats scurried like a magician's assistant toward Mrs. Sharply. She carried two Folgers cans decorated in pink and blue glitter. Mrs. Sharply set down her sugar, taking the cans from the aide and giving each a good shake. From the pink can, the first name she pulled was Mimi Yazzie, who stood and slinked forward, burying her face into her arms as Mrs. Sharply called out her partner, Mike Ramos. This cycle of humiliation lasted for several more rounds before I was partnered with Roberto Martinez, the bone boy.

After school, Robbie and I sat outside on the swings. He was a scrawny kid with frequently chapped lips and a light dusting of freckles across his low nose. He played soccer and always wore a beat-up blue windbreaker and knockoff Adidas sneakers, with four stripes instead of three. The sugar baby was planted snug in his lap, balanced ever so gently between his two stick-arms. His dark eyes were so big and wide they resembled two brown pigeon eggs and he spoke with a quavering, squeaky voice. "They said we have to name it. Do you want to pick it out, Sierra?"

"No, you name it." I swung up. "And you take it home tonight." I swung down. "I'll watch it tomorrow, but only if I have to."

"That's cool," he said. "What about Miranda? That's my grandma's name."

"Whatever," I sighed, leaning back on the swing. "Name it after your grandmother. Name it after your entire family. I don't care." I pumped until the rusted chain pulled taut. Then I jumped, landing in the mushy gravel with both feet. I took off for home.

"Ain't that something," my father said as he and I ate breakfast the next morning. On our small black-and-white TV above the microwave, aerial shots of the dig site were being shown on the news. The land appeared as an enormous shadow box with scraps of ancient people instead of thimbles and porcelain knickknacks.

"Can we go see it?" I asked, spooning my last bit of cornflakes into my mouth.

"I suspect they don't want us to do that," he said, keeping his eyes to the TV. There were deep lines around his eyelids, his hair was purely silver, and his hands were spotted from years of working as a roofer beneath the Colorado sun. People had begun to mistake him for my grandfather.

"Why not? We should be allowed to." I walked to the sink and tossed my dirty dish inside. "It's where we're from. It's *our* people."

My father scratched his chin. There was a thin turquoise ring on his finger where there had once been a gold wedding band. "Don't leave a dish in the sink," he said. "How many times I got to tell you that, Sierra?"

I turned back and soaped up my bowl. "I mean it. I want to go."

"Things like this have always happened around here. It's nothing special."

I told him it was new to me as I scrubbed my dish with a green and yellow sponge, the milky water gargling loudly down the drain's black rubber lips. As I rinsed the bowl once more, I peered through the window above the sink. The morning was clear and in the distance the mountains were crystal blue like an enormous wave. As if sailing across those waters, a small white pickup truck with a front-end bra pulled down our street and rumbled over the gravel in our driveway. Long dark hair clouded the truck's windshield and very red and very long fingernails were coiled around the steering wheel. A silver rosary dangled above the dash.

"Papa," I called over my shoulder, drying my hands on my jeans.

My father rose and stood tall behind me, smelling of leather and dirt. "Looks like she's back again." He grunted some, swishing spit around inside his mouth before shooting a stream of yolky bile into the sink. "Go outside, Sierra. Say hello to your mother."

My mother first left three years earlier. It happened one morning after she cooked breakfast. I watched as she gathered her keys and coat and walked into our wintry yard without any shoes. She left footprints as slight as bird tracks in the snow. When I asked my father later why she had left, he simply said,

"Sometimes a person's unhappiness can make them forget they are a part of something bigger, something like a family, a people, even a tribe."

My mother occasionally would come home for a day or two to gather forgotten necklaces or purses, though over time my father moved her things from the bedroom to a box in the crawl space. Her visits were infrequent enough that I learned to live without her. It wasn't easy at first. Sometimes I'd hear a funny story at school or church and my first thought would be, *You have to tell Mama.* But over time that urge to be with her, to tell her things, to be a part of her, it went away. Just like she always did.

On my mother's first night back, she couldn't find an apron so she made dinner in one of my father's old T-shirts. With the kitchen TV up loud on *Entertainment Tonight,* she cooked pork chops sizzled in their own fat and smothered in green chili. Whenever I'd glance up from my math homework on the coffee table, I'd catch glimpses of her in the kitchen rummaging through junk drawers and cabinets. I wondered what she was searching for and thought to offer my help, but I realized I didn't care if my mother found anything in our home again.

When she finally called my father and me to the big table, I pulled my sugar sack—Miranda Martinez-Cordova—from my backpack. "Dinnertime," I whispered, admiring the face I had given her with a Sharpie. Her eyes were big and wide with short lines for lashes. Her mouth was a blissfully flat smirk.

"Your favorite," my mother said, handing a plate to my father. He casually spun it above his head and eased into his seat at the table. The two of them were acting as if nothing had happened, as if my mother had always been there cooking in the kitchen. I felt like my father was a liar, someone who could pretend everything was fine when, really, how could he be anything but sad?

"Do you want something to drink, Sierra?" asked my mother.

"No," I said, covering Miranda's mouth. "I don't want anything."

"Nonsense," said my mother. "You're becoming a woman. Women need vitamins and nutrients. You'll have some milk."

My mother opened a cupboard, the small one beside the stove where the glasses had once been, but my father corrected her with a flick of his knife. "Left of the sink."

My mother tilted her head and steadied her mouth into a tight smile. After pouring the milk, she placed the glass in front of me and quickly glanced at Miranda. Robbie had dressed her in one of his little sister's old striped pink onesies. "Does your doll want a plate?"

"She's not a doll. And she's way too young for solids."

My mother laughed and took her seat, closing her eyes while my father led us in prayer. Miranda and I kept our eyes open. My mother had taken off the old T-shirt and wore a blue dress with white-embroidered flowers that had many loose threads. Her lips were thinner and her black hair was shorter than I remembered. She used to only wear silver, but she had on a gold necklace, the thin braided chain glowing against her bronze skin.

After we said amen, my parents made the sign of the cross and my mother opened her reddish-brown eyes. Her eye makeup appeared as a buildup of silt. "You know," she said, turning to me, "I thought we were out of salt. I was going to have you run next door to ask Mrs. Kelly if we could borrow some."

"She's dead." I hunched down and rested my chin on Miranda's head.

"What?"

"She's not alive anymore."

My father gently said, "Old Mrs. Kelly passed away last winter, Josie."

My mother mouthed an "Oh" and looked at her plate. She briskly apologized and we continued dinner in silence. Above us the ceiling fan spun in rapid circles, slicing the air, sending waves of coolness over each of us. My mother and father kept glancing at one another—smiling, chewing, smiling, sipping, and smiling some more. After some time, I got sick of their cheeriness and gulped the last of my milk. Then, as loud as possible, I slammed my empty glass on the table.

"So, *Josie*," I said, "what brings you down from Denver? Or do you normally drive around cooking pork chops for people?"

"Sierra," my father barked. "Don't you call your mother by her first name." He shook his head and I avoided his strict gaze.

My mother smiled sweetly. "Tell me about all those Indian graves the boys from your school found out west."

My stomach suddenly lurched with the sounds of digestive failure. "I don't know anything about it," I said, stroking Miranda.

"Sure you do," my father interjected. "That Roberto Martinez, the boy who found the bones, he's your partner for that sugar thing. Your school project."

"To think," my mother said. "This whole time those bones were right in Saguarita beneath our feet."

"That's not true," I said. "They weren't beneath *your* feet."

She giggled a bit. "I was here for a long while, Sierra. I think I know a thing or two about Saguarita."

Though I wanted to tell her she didn't know about anything, I turned my face to my lap and went quiet. After dinner, I sat in my room, where I pressed my ear against the cool white door.

Muffled and low, I could hear my father in the living room ask my mother about her drive—road conditions, springtime flurries, if the mountain goats hobbled along the pass. He didn't ask why she was back or if she missed us—questions that hurt me to think about. I moved away from the door and tossed Miranda into the corner.

"She cried all night. I didn't get any sleep," I told Robbie the next morning as I shoved Miranda into his arms. We met outside thirty minutes before school in our usual spot by the swings. It was chilly and the air smelled like pancake breakfast and frost.

"How could she cry?" he asked. "She's only sugar."

The sun was coming up. The light leaked over the land in velvety streaks of pinks and golds. My mother once told me this meant the angels were baking cookies. "Isn't that what babies do? Cry and crap themselves and cry some more?"

"Hey," Robbie said, his chapped mouth bunched to the side. "Where's her outfit?"

"Lost it."

Robbie sighed and bent down to his backpack. He pulled a diaper from the front mesh pocket. "Give her here. We'll lose points if she's wearing the same diaper from last night." He lay Miranda on the loose gravel and frowned at the new sad, sleepy face I had given her that morning. Her eyelashes were tarantula-like and her mouth was downturned. Robbie fumbled with the diaper, applying and reapplying the adhesive sides.

"So," I said, standing above him, "what was it like?"

"What was what like, Sierra?"

"Finding those dead people. Was it scary?"

Robbie got the diaper to stick. He patted Miranda's black

marker face and stood up with a bounce. "Not scary," he said. "But it was weird, you know? We've lived here our whole lives and no one knew about all this old stuff in the ground."

"I guess," I said, thinking of the piñon trees where my father had hung a bluish hammock in our yard. Their roots, he said, had undoubtedly grazed the dead bodies of our ancestors, both Spanish and Indian. I used to play in the shade of those piñons, cracking their nuts with two rocks held firmly in my hands. After pulling away the hard shells, I'd toss the spongy insides into my mouth. I didn't swallow them, though. I was afraid of letting any amount of death, from the soil or elsewhere, work its way into me. "Everything is old here. I mean *everything*."

Robbie nodded. He was rocking Miranda back and forth in such a way I'd only seen small girls do with dolls. "I heard your mom's back again. My grandma saw her buying pork chops at Rainbow Market."

I kicked at the gravel, scuffing my Mary Janes. Dust flew between us. "The bitch is back."

Robbie pretended to cover Miranda's ears. "Dude," he said, "don't call your mom a bitch. What if Miranda called you a bitch?"

"Guess it's a good thing babies can't talk," I said. "Especially ones made of sugar."

Robbie was smiling and had lifted Miranda into the air. He briefly held her against the sky before bringing her back down. "Remember when your mom was our group leader for Day on the Prairie?"

"Yeah," I said, lowering my voice.

"And we all got lost looking for that old barn she said was haunted? Then she let us eat three packs of Oreos? And you had to go to the bathroom in the bushes." Robbie laughed, but I frowned and he quickly turned serious. "Why is she back this time?"

The school bell sounded. Class was starting in ten minutes. We reached for our backpacks and walked toward the front doors. I lifted Miranda from Robbie's arms. "Who knows with that woman? Maybe she wants to see the dig site. Or maybe she likes taking vacations to her old life."

Within a week, my mother blended into our home as well as Miranda did. Which is to say, not very well at all. When it was just my father, he worked late and usually only had time to heat up a frozen pizza or fix a box of macaroni. Our small purple house was often messy, though we each had a chore list that was conquered by Sunday. With my mother back, the home took on a new order, a different rhythm. She cooked unhealthy but comforting foods, the house constantly emitting a pungent odor of bacon grease and red chili powder. Other times she cleaned. She'd twirl around with a broom, swaying her hips to the music on the radio—an oldies station or some honky-tonk crap. Most evenings, after my father came home from work, he'd unlace his boots in the foyer and then move his arm along my mother's slight waist. Together they'd rock back and forth to the music. It was nauseating.

Each day after school, I'd come home to discover that my mother had made my bed and placed my stuffed animals in a dog pile above my pillows. I'd immediately throw them to the floor. With a detergent that reeked of artificial springtime and cottony clouds, she also did my laundry, taking the time to match my socks, a luxury I hadn't experienced in years. One afternoon, as I sat on the couch, my feet covered in those matching socks and kicked up on the armrest, my mother walked by and swiped them down like she was swatting a fly. "What're you doing inside? It's a beautiful day." Her arms were planted firmly at her sides. She wore a brightly colored tunic and black leggings, making her appear like a 1960s glamour model. She was young still, only in her mid-thirties.

"It's hotter than a pig's armpit out there." I craned my neck, looking past her at the television. An Herbal Essence shampoo commercial was on and long-haired women were moaning under waterfalls.

"You have such a foul mouth," my mother said. "And pigs don't have armpits, genius." She began lifting sofa pillows as though searching for something. "Hey, where's that sugar bag you carry around? Your little baby for school."

"She's with her father. He has her until the weekend."

"Oh," my mother said. "Well, get up off this sofa. We're going for a drive."

I couldn't remember the last time I had been alone with my mother in a car. "What? Where to?"

She smiled, the seams of her mouth running with red lipstick. "You'll see."

We parked on a steep hill overlooking the dig site. Below us archaeologists in white hats and khaki shorts swarmed the gutted earth like invasive ants. The plot was as long and wide as a shallow public swimming pool and was divvied up into human-size squares. The sky was cloudless and blue, except for the sun's golden orb. At the horizon, there was a crashing display of earth and air. My mother stood before me and held her arms out, flapping them as if they were useless wings. Wind blew her hair, twirling the strands around her face, hiding her eyes behind sections of black. For the first time since she'd come home,

I remembered how beautiful I once found her to be. As a little girl, I'd play dress-up in her satin nightdresses and lacy bras, admiring their slight weight and wondering if I'd ever own clothes like that.

"What do you think?" she asked. "Isn't it pretty?"

I shrugged and stood beside her. The wind carried her jasmine scent.

"Ever feel like the land is swallowing you whole, Sierra? That all of this beauty is wrapped around you so tight it's like being in a rattlesnake's mouth?"

"I see this all the time," I said. "And I don't feel like I'm being eaten alive by anything."

My mother gave me a sideways glance. "You will someday. Maybe it'll come later for you than it did for me. Children tend to do that. Marriage. Life. All these things." Moving behind me, she hunched down and slipped her cold hands over my eyes. "Try it. Close your eyes and hold your arms against the wind. You'll feel it."

I allowed my arms to float up and coast. A kaleidoscope of images spun against my closed lids. I saw the day when I was ten years old, right before my mother left for the first time. She took me to the pueblo where her grandmother was born in New Mexico. Holding my hand, my mother walked us through a small adobe church. She touched the pews with the tips of her red nails as we moved closer to the altar. We stepped into a side room where we lit white candles with long, slim sticks. My mother sent prayers for all those she loved into the sky with smoke, but I sent only one. *Please,* I pleaded to the Virgin, *don't let my mother cry anymore.* I was sick of finding her silently weeping, the sobs bobbing in her throat—at the stove, in the bathtub, kneeling in the dead garden beside our house.

When I opened my eyes, my mother was beside me, a strange blank expression on her face. "Did you feel it?" she asked.

"No," I said. "I didn't feel anything." Goose pimples rose on my neck and arms. "It's just windy and cold."

"All right, Sierra. Then let's get home. I'll start dinner."

As she headed for her pickup, I looked over the hill's edge and down into the dig site once more. The archaeologists were huddled in small groups. The rich odor of disrupted earth blew into me. Everything was terrifyingly silent. I thought about how quiet the world could sound and how when I stood there beside my mother, for a moment, I was afraid she had left me on the hillside, stranded forever.

"Xerophthalmia," Mrs. Sharply said, "is one of many child-hood diseases your babies could get." It was the following Monday, the final week of sugar babies. Another assembly was being held in the gym. Two kids in front of me had swaddled their baby in a blanket, while others around us had glued on googly eyes and red yarn mouths. Robbie sat beside me with Miranda. She looked exceptionally fashionable. That morning I had wrapped a quilted pillowcase around her like a muumuu dress.

"Among other things," Mrs. Sharply continued, "xeroph-thalmia is a vitamin A deficiency which makes it so a person can't produce tears."

I leaned over to Robbie. "I wish you had that disease. Then you'd stop whining about me drawing on Miranda." I had re-cently drawn crucifixes and anchors across her back. Tattoos, I called them, but Robbie said she looked like a bathroom wall.

"She's a baby," he whispered with closed eyes. "Babies don't need tattoos."

"Sugar," I said. "She is a bag of sugar."

"Now think for a moment," Mrs. Sharply said, waving both arms into the air. "Think of all the times you cry. Sometimes they are happy, and, sometimes, they are sad. But crying is natural. Take a moment to remember the last time *you* cried."

The gymnasium went silent. Only the hiss of the fluorescent lights above us could be heard. Students hung their heads, as if possessed by their darkest, most sorrowful memories. I waited for the other students to finish reminiscing about their dear old dead grandparents and broken bones.

"Now, parents," said Mrs. Sharply, "you can see that not being able to cry would be an awful condition. For homework, we will each need to research a childhood disease. Tomorrow we will draw diseases from a hat. Some babies will get a disease, but—just like in life—some will not. It's the luck of the draw."

Later that day, Robbie hurried after me as I walked home. His backpack seemed comically wider than he did. "You have to take Miranda," he said. "I have soccer tonight." From the giant backpack, he scooped Miranda out, slowly handing her over. She was somehow heavier than usual.

"What the heck have you been feeding her?" I asked.

Robbie petted her belly. "That was weird, Mrs. Sharply asking about crying."

"She's a real wacko," I said, hoisting Miranda on my hip. The sky was endlessly blue with paper wisps of clouds. I caught myself tilting Miranda up to see. "So, when was it, Robbie? The last time you cried?"

"That's sort of personal, Sierra."

"Roberto Martinez, I'm your child's mother. I deserve to know these things."

"All right." Robbie took a deep breath. "After I found the bones, that night I woke up and thought I saw a skeleton woman at the foot of my bed. I didn't know who she was, but later my grandma told me it was Doña Sebastiana, the lady version of the grim reaper. Death."

"You cried from a bad dream?"

"No, Sierra. It was more than that." Robbie scratched his head and his scalp sounded sandy. "What about you? When's the last time you cried?"

I peered down the block at my little purple house. My mother's pickup wasn't in the driveway and I figured she had gone to Rainbow Market for more pork chops, but for a moment something in my chest ached, a gnawing worry that she was gone again, this time for good. I broke into a sprint and ran toward home. "I don't cry," I called over my shoulder. "Only little girls and babies do that."

"I have some new tattoo ideas," I said to Miranda, who sat on the kitchen table, stiffly leaning to the left in a column of sunlight. I was sifting through the junk drawer looking for markers. I had opened every window and for the first time in days the house didn't smell like pork. It reeked with the richness of the mountains and desert, rain and sage and cedar pulled together as one. When I realized the drawer only had rubber bands and dead batteries, I said, "Don't worry, you little sack of cavities. I have some markers in my room."

I crawled beneath my bed, over the uncrushed carpet, surrounded by gobs of lint and balled hair. I was looking for a shoe box filled with art supplies, but I ended up fishing out my PRIVATE PROPERTY box instead, the place where I kept movie ticket stubs, old diaries, and birthday cards from my mother. She made the cards herself and I imagined her in some sunny apartment in downtown Denver. Houseplants and cacti lined the windows while filtered city light fell upon her at the sofa licking stamps and writing out her old address.

Sitting on my floor, my legs spread and the birthday cards dumped around me like confetti, I ran my fingers over their sharp edges and smooth ribbons. I came upon one from my eleventh birthday, the first card my mother sent after she left. I held the purple and gold paper in my palm, then opened the card as if it were the warm, beating heart of an animal. My mother had placed three marigolds inside and they nearly crumbled in my hands.

*To my baby, Sierra. Today is your birthday, and when you were born, I knew everything would change, that every day would be your day, that nothing would be the same.*

I climbed onto my bed, where I nestled into Miranda. "See this," I said. "This is from *my* mom." I looked at her sad face, and, for a split second, I imagined Miranda as a real infant, a baby who breathed and cried. I rolled her to my lips and dryly kissed her forehead. "I don't know if I'm very nice to you," I whispered.

I then caught a glimpse of my mother standing in the doorway. She was leaning into the wall, limp and fragile. Her reddish-brown eyes were without makeup and her hair was stacked in a sloppy pile on top of her head. "You're good with her."

"She isn't real," I said.

My mother stepped toward me, moving gracefully in her

skin. She sat on the foot of my bed with very straight posture and stiff arms. She seemed nervous—the way cats stiffen their backs before danger strikes. "It's sort of strange they make you kids do this. You're only thirteen, but I can understand how they think it prepares you, I suppose. Not that having a sack of sugar for two weeks would prepare anyone for a new life."

I pulled Miranda closer and wiggled my thumb over her quilted midsection.

"I'm not sure if anyone is prepared for raising a child. It doesn't seem to be something we can practice before it actually happens."

I shrugged and rolled Miranda onto my belly. "Where did you go today?"

My mother stared straight ahead, her eyes glassy. "For a drive through the canyon. Would you believe it? I saw two hawks. They were playing in the wind."

Hawks were common in Saguarita. We had an entire unit in sixth grade about them. They danced before mating, could dive 150 miles per hour, stayed with one partner all their lives. I was surprised that my mother paid them any attention. "What kinds of birds do you see in the city?" I asked.

"Crows," said my mother. "Just a bunch of crows." She paused, tracing Miranda's eyelashes with her long red nails. "How long do you have her?"

"A few more days," I said, rubbing Miranda's back slowly. "I can't wait to get rid of this thing. She's so annoying."

"Imagine someday when it's a real baby. It will be much harder."

"That's the point," I said. "Miranda isn't real. If she was, I'd be a lot nicer to her, like Robbie is. He's better at taking care of her."

My mother folded her hands neatly in her lap. She kneaded

her fingers back and forth and a trickle of sadness moved between us like a static shock. "Can you believe that when you were born I was only three years older than you are now?" She forced a laugh, dropped her gaze to the carpet. "I had to stop going to school."

"Did you miss it?" I asked.

My mother sighed and considered my question for a long time. "I didn't know I could miss school. I thought I was just sad, but I take classes now. At a community college. You could go there someday."

My mother went quiet. She pulled the rubber band from her head, allowing her hair to unravel around her shoulders and neck. She looked gloriously dark and light at the same time. There was a shining glint in her brown eyes. She looked younger. She looked happy. "I bet you'll be an artist someday, Sierra." My mother pointed to the tattoos across Miranda's back, "That's what I wanted to be." She smiled and we both laughed.

"Here," she said. "Let me braid your hair. I can do a tight one that will last for a few days."

I pulled away at first but soon moved back toward my mother. I was ashamed of myself that I still wanted her close to me, even after everything she had done. I eventually rested my head in her chilly hands and tried to forget how bad my mother had hurt me. Her fingers wove through my hair like she was sewing a quilt. I nearly fell asleep in her arms as I held Miranda in my own. Lying there with my mother in the afternoon light of my bedroom, I imagined her far into the future, driving day and night, her little white truck sliding from mountain peak to valley, through snow and heat waves, windstorms and lightning. Her headlights beam bright and warm, shining into town, the place where I'll live when I'm finally a grown-up and my mother's black hair is silver and her face is well lined. In the distance, I see her arriving, joyously waving to me, her last stop.

When I woke up the next morning, my father was alone at the kitchen table eating oatmeal and reading the newspaper. Part of me wanted to ask where my mother was, but I knew she was already heading north over the pass, back to that sunny apartment of hers in Denver. Even her chair was gone from the table. My father scooted a bowl of cereal toward me. He then smacked the paper with his hand. "I'll be damned," he said. "Those Indians on the ridge, they got some formal petition going. They're closing up the dig site." His eyes met mine over the top of the paper. "Sorry I didn't take you to see it, Sierra. There will be another one someday."

"I did see it," I said. "Mama took me."

My father swallowed hard and shook out the paper. It sounded like rain. "Want some orange juice with your breakfast? I got the kind without pulp that you like."

"No, Papa," I said, "I'm not feeling too good. Would it be okay if I stayed home from school?"

He raised his white eyebrows. They reflected the low sunlight pouring into the kitchen through the sheer curtains above the sink. "If you feel that bad, then of course you can."

I spent most of the day in bed with Miranda cupped in my arms. We listened to the radio perched on my windowsill. The country songs my mother liked filled the small bedroom and every now and then I'd lean over with Miranda close to my chest and feel like crying. Then, at three o'clock, there was a quick knock on the door.

Robbie stood on my stoop covered in a mist of sweat around his temples and beneath his mouth.

"What're you doing here?" I asked. "And why are you out of breath? Did you skip or something?"

He wagged his head back and forth. "It's awful, Sierra. Just awful."

"I'm sure you're a wonderful skipper. Don't be so hard on yourself."

"No, not that. It's Miranda." He hunched over and took a huge breath. "She's dead."

"Miranda can't die, moron."

Robbie peered at me, a deep sadness in his gaze. "We pulled diseases out of a hat today. Most kids didn't get anything bad. Some got chicken pox. But Miranda, she got SIDS. If you don't know what that is because you didn't do your homework, it means sudden infant death syndrome."

"I know what SIDS is," I said. "What are we supposed to do now? Throw her away?"

"But we can't," Robbie whined. "It's Miranda."

I stared at him for a long while, counting how many times he blinked without tears rolling out of his eyes. Then I said, "I have an idea."

Robbie and I parked our bikes near the edge of the hill overlooking the dig site. I had wrapped Miranda in a black pillowcase. She resembled a baby nun. I pulled her from my handlebar basket and one last time arched her face to the heavens. There was a mass of gray clouds. They spread evenly over the land like a patchwork of fog. "Look," I whispered. "Even the sky is sad for you."

Robbie stood beside me at the border between the hill and the dig site. He reached out with a thin chicken wing of an arm and patted Miranda softly on the head. We stood at the edge of the hill for some time, listening to the grumbling moans of the clouds and the far-off crackling of thunder. I picked out a spot easy to aim for in the middle of the pit. Then, tipping back, I readied myself to launch Miranda above my head with both arms, but Robbie stopped me. "You're going to throw Miranda in there?"

"What else can we do?"

With those big sad eyes, he looked into the dig site. Then he looked at me. "I can kick her farther."

"You're going to kick our baby into her grave?" The wind carried my voice away from me as if it wasn't my own to begin with.

"I play soccer, Sierra."

Taking her from my arms, he delicately set Miranda on the edge of the hill, her limp body leaning mostly to the left. He backed up a few steps, and then pushed himself forward with huge strides, his arms flying. When his tennis shoe made contact with Miranda, her body lifted from the earth as though she was nothing more than a helium balloon. She twirled in the air as her sugar insides spiraled out of her body from a hole Robbie's foot had torn in the bag. The sugar blew with the wind, sprinkling the dirt with bits of white. How pretty, I thought, and she landed with a thud.

# SABRINA
# & CORINA

. . . . . . . . . . . . . . . .

My grandmother called with the news. Though I wasn't entirely surprised, I had to ask her four times to repeat herself. "Strangled," she said over the phone. "That's how it happened."

I was doing makeup at Macy's at the time, and after finishing my last face of the day, I drove to her house, where my youngest cousins played tag in the yard. I made my way past them through the chain-link gate, holding my purse above my head as they yelled my name and swirled around me, trying to get me to join their game. Inside, in the front room, my father was splayed out on the couch with a Rockies cap pulled over his eyes. One of my uncles leaned beside him, lightly clutching the remote. Another sat motionless on an old recliner, his eyes to his glowing cellphone. From the back bedroom came the howling cries of Sabrina's mother. The men flinched but carried on watching the muted television screen. No one acknowledged my arrival.

. . . . . . .

In the kitchen, my grandmother stirred three restaurant-size steel pots with a wooden spoon. Her nails were golden and long and her silver hair was up, bouffant style. I had experienced enough Cordova deaths to know one pot was filled with green chili, another with pintos, and the last one with menudo. Deaths, weddings, birthdays—the menu was always the same. "Here," my grandmother said, pointing with the spoon to a mound of raw pork on the table. "Make yourself useful."

I took my place among the women. My mother and I silently chopped the pork into small pieces for the chili. One of my aunties made a pitcher of lemonade, another chopped onions, and another readied plates of food for the men. We worked quickly and silently, shouldering past one another in the small kitchen. A few cousins sat Indian style on the linoleum floor, sorting through a Payless shoe box of family photos. They passed around photos of Sabrina as though they had suddenly forgotten how she looked. *Such thick, long black hair,* they said. *Look at her blue eyes in this one.* They had always admired Sabrina, copying her makeup and her clothes. She was the family beauty, the gorgeous cousin, their lovely doll. It was only a matter of time, I thought, before they emulated her in other ways. One of them had already been suspended for showing up to math class drunk from the night before. She had been with a boy, her knees were bleeding. My youngest cousin gazed at a photo of Sabrina bikini clad along the creek in Boulder. "What a pretty figure," she said, pinching her own stomach and sulking.

I carried the cutting board to the stove and pushed the pork into a skillet. My grandmother stood beside me, smelling of Vicks and the Chanel No. 5 samples I had given her from work. She looked at me with her tiny brown eyes iced over with bluish cataracts. I wondered how she saw anything. She stirred the pork until the chunks were browned and then submerged them in the chili, little by little, with her wooden spoon.

"You knew her best," she said abruptly, still staring into the pot, her tone like an accusation directed toward anyone. "You knew her best, *Corina*."

The other women stopped what they were doing. They stared at me, their ears nearly rising out of the strands of their black hair, wolflike, as they waited for my response. I didn't tell them I hadn't seen or spoken to Sabrina in months, and by that time, she wasn't the Sabrina I knew anymore. I placed the cutting board in the sink and washed my hands.


When I was eleven and Sabrina was twelve, we crawled barefoot out of our grandmother's attic window and stood on the roof above the porch. Though it was nearly fully dark, under our feet the shingles still felt warm from the evening sun. We took in the view of Denver's budding skyline from my grandmother's Westside neighborhood. Skyscrapers rose like granite cliffs, whitish and bleak against the night. Our family's church, St. Joseph's, stood nearby on the corner of Sixth Avenue, bells ringing as indoor lights twinkled through stained-glass windows.

We lay down, our hair spreading between us, our arms folded beneath our necks. Above us, miles into the sky, an airplane's red light coasted through the dark. Sabrina held her left hand in front of her face, moving it closer to her eyes and then further away. Her nails were sparkly blue and the friendship bracelet I had made for her moved up her wrist. "What's your first memory in the entire world?" she asked.

"I can't remember."

She lightly slapped my arm. "Try."

I closed my eyes and I saw Sabrina and myself as babies near a mountain lake beneath a blanket the color of marigolds with plastic mirrors woven into the fabric. The blanket caught and held light, as if covered in a small portion of the sun. A honeybee floated down from the cloudless sky, landing on my cheek.

"It's probably that time I got stung by a bee," I said. "We were little and with our moms in the mountains."

Sabrina squinted into the murky night. Very few stars were visible, and there was no moon. "You're such a copycat, Corina. That was me. I was the one who got stung."

"No way," I said. "I felt it. It burned me all the way through my face and neck."

She sat upright and with closed eyes shook her head. "Go ask our moms. I'm the one who was hurt."

Around eleven, the men began snoring on the couch and the little cousins had passed out like sloppy drunks on the floor. The women made funeral plans in the kitchen. All of us were there except Sabrina's mother, who had taken a Xanax and fallen asleep in my grandmother's bed. The rosary and viewing would be held in two days at Ramirez Mortuary. The funeral Mass would be the following morning, then a short trip to the cemetery, and a reception afterward in the church's basement. One of my cousins said she could get us a deal on a karaoke DJ, but fortunately another cousin told her she was a tacky idiot.

We couldn't agree on a closed casket. My grandmother was against it. She spoke of funerals where an outdated picture of the departed was presented to a room of teary-eyed mourners. "Nothing like that," she said. "It's so phony, disrespectful.

With no body to view, it's like they never were on this earth to begin with."

"It might be better that way," my mother said. "Carlos at the mortuary said her neck looks awful, real ugly and swollen."

"He's just being lazy," said my grandmother. "Carlos can do all sorts of things these days with the new creams and chemicals."

One of my aunties groaned and reminded everyone that last fall, after Auntie Celia passed away peacefully in her sleep, Carlos made her face look like a pickled pig's ear. "I can only imagine what he'll do to Sabrina," she added.

"If you're all so worried about it, Carlos doesn't have to do it." My grandmother pointed in my direction. "Corina can."

"Do what, Grandma?" I asked stunned. "Her makeup?"

"Yes, jita, and her hair. That's your job."

I thought of the quinceañera the previous winter, where my wrists felt like they'd fall off after I did makeup and hair for eleven cousins and their friends. I had been encouraged to learn cosmetology partly because I was good at it and partly, I suspected, because my family loved free services and products. "I know you get them samples," my aunties would say. "Hook us up with some lipstick or that antiwrinkle cream. That shit's so expensive."

"I don't do makeovers on dead people," I said.

"Nonsense." My grandmother smacked the table. "Put the makeup on Sabrina and make sure she looks good. Pay special attention to her neck."

"I couldn't do that. I wouldn't know how."

My grandmother looked at her lap and then at the stove. Her throat trembled and she wiped her face. It was as close to crying as she ever got. She turned back to me and I knew to say yes.

———

Sabrina loved our grandmother's house. She especially loved the bathroom. The lighting was warm and rosy and on each of the four walls was a full-length mirror. My grandmother believed every woman needed to know how she looked from any angle. It was important, she said, to know how the rest of the world viewed us.

When Sabrina and I were in middle school, she stole a pair of heart-shaped sunglasses from the dollar store by shoving them into her sock. The next time we were both at our grandmother's house, she wore them all day, fluttering around like some starlet, flicking her wrist and puffing out her hair. At one point, she convinced me to climb onto the bathroom's pink countertop with her. She had us turn our bodies so we faced one another, our legs bent in the bowl of the sink. All around we were reflected in the four mirrors endlessly, like one tangled spider of a girl.

"I think," Sabrina said, making a kissy-face at herself, "that I could be a model or an actress."

Her face was a delicate oval with high cheekbones and a heavy bottom lip. But her most noticeable feature, her eyes, was covered by the sunglasses. Their pale blue color alone was striking, but the shape of them—very round and wide—is what made them unusual. Even strangers on the street said she resembled a living doll. "We should move to Cali when we're older," I said. "Become movie stars."

"We should." Sabrina clapped her hands. "I can be like Salma Hayek or go blond and be a real bombshell."

"Blond? Who wants to be blond?"

"My dad was a blond. At least, he was in those pictures my mom has." Sabrina often mentioned these photos, the only glimpse either of us had seen of her father. He took off before she was born. My grandmother told me he was a nobody—some white guy with a name like a stuffy nose, Stuart or Randal.

"I don't care if your dad was blond. You look better with hair like me and our moms. You'd look adopted if you had stringy yellow hair."

"And I don't look adopted now? Not even with my blue eyes?"

"No way. You look like a Cordova," I said. "So, if you're Salma Hayek, who am I? Which actress?"

A look of deep concentration came over Sabrina's face. She smiled. "You can be my personal assistant."

"You wish," I said. "What about Dolores del Rio?"

"Who the heck is that?"

"She's from Grandma's old-time movies. The kind without words."

Sabrina slid the heart-shaped sunglasses off her face, her eyes bright beneath them. "That's just dumb. No one wants a girl who doesn't talk. You might as well be dead."


Ramirez Mortuary was on the corner of a busy intersection north of downtown, an undistinguished house with reflective windows and plastic marigolds lining the cement pathway to the entrance. Nothing about it, inside or out, had changed much over the years. The carpet was still seafoam green, the walls still creamy pastel, and the sofa in the sitting area, where I was to meet Carlos, was still bubble gum pink.

I sat down and glanced through some pamphlets on loss and grief spread over a glass coffee table. They all had glossy photos of beautiful white-haired people with pinched features and light eyes. Sabrina would have looked like that, had she grown old. Our cousins used to give her a hard time. "With eyes like that," they'd say, "you look like one of those dogs. A husky or maybe a wolf." My grandmother told Sabrina to ignore them. She said people will find the loveliest part of you and try to make it ugly. "And they will do anything," she always said, "to own that piece of you."

"I can spot a Cordova from a mile away," Carlos said, marching toward me, one hand on his hip, a short man with a thin mustache and a paisley western shirt. His black hair had thinned since I last saw him at Auntie Celia's funeral.

I tossed the pamphlets back onto the table and handed him a duffel bag of Sabrina's things—a modest red dress, a quartz rosary, silk flowers for her hair, an old photograph. "Like you asked for. I didn't bring any shoes, though. My grandma told me you wouldn't need those."

"Dead people," he said, "are like white people. They can't dance."

I laughed a little. "You make that one up?"

"Oh, yes, honey. That's how it goes."

He led me down a carpeted hallway with yolk-colored squares. After my godfather died of hepatitis in the early nineties, Sabrina and I used those squares to play hopscotch. At the end of the hallway, he opened a door to a showroom of caskets. Many were dark wood, some shiny metal, and a few radiantly white. In the corner were smaller versions, for children. Carlos leaned against the smallest one. "Before we head into the other room, I want to go over some things."

I nodded.

"Number one, if you don't want to do this, you don't have to. Number two, you have two hours. The wake starts then. And number three, this is a favor for your grandmother. Don't tell anyone I let you do this."

"So, that's it? There's nothing else?"

· · · · · · ·

"Wait here. I'll go ahead and put on her dress. I'll call you in when the body's ready." Carlos pulled a set of keys from the retractable chain on his belt. Before opening the door, he said, "And I'm sorry about Sabrina. She was a beautiful girl. Really, she was."

We were inseparable in high school. Sabrina was my best friend, my closest cousin. My father would give me a hard time, ask if I ever tired of carrying her deadweight, but Sabrina was fun. She was vivid and felt everything deeply, from heartbreak to the drunken nights we stayed up until 4:00 A.M., mapping out our tiny lives with enormity only Sabrina could imagine. To her, everything was possible—money, true love, a way out of Colorado. Even after she dropped out in eleventh grade to work at a sports bar downtown, I used to do homework in a back booth, marveling at the way she glided between tables, sleek and fluid with her long hair curled around her elegant neck. Men would follow her between their bites of onion rings and beer-battered fish, insatiable, as if my cousin was just another symptom of their hunger.

After graduation, my father offered to pay for cosmetology school. He said that I needed to do something besides run around like other Cordova women. He mostly meant Sabrina, of course, who by that point had started showing up to family dinners smelling like a barroom floor. But it wasn't just her. There was the distant niece whose infant son was taken away by the state, the cousins who died messing around with heroin, Great-Auntie Doty left blind after a date with the wrong man, and Auntie Liz, found dead in her Chrysler, the motor running and the garage door locked. My grandmother hardly mentioned Auntie Liz except to say that what killed her had killed them all.

While I was studying cuts and colors, perms and relaxers, Sabrina continued working in bars and sleeping with men who all looked alike: tall, thick-necked, green eyes or blue. In my mind, these men formed a lineup of indifferent masculine faces, a continuation of the withdrawn expression I had seen in those old photographs of Sabrina's father. Sometimes she'd visit me at the beauty college. She would stand at my station in wrinkled clothes, looking like she'd just woken up at noon. While the other girls snickered and popped their gum, Sabrina would scoop away her hair and I'd see the bruises, hickeys like rotten goose eggs down her throat. "They'll send me home from work," she'd say, and I'd always help her conceal everything.

After finishing beauty school, I rented a studio apartment on the Westside that overlooked an abandoned public pool. At night, on my second-floor balcony, I'd sit and wonder about the missing diving board, replaced with an orange traffic cone, as if that could stop someone from leaping headlong into hard cement. It was a lonely place, and Sabrina only visited during the rare times when she was single. She'd come over and shadow me throughout the apartment, like a child who was afraid she'd stop existing if someone wasn't there to see her.

"You ever do makeovers on women who look hideous without makeup?"

She was sitting on the lid of my toilet with two Coronas between her thighs, one for each of us. We had the radio on an oldies station, the type of music our mothers played when we were little girls and they would drive us through the mountains in summertime.

"Sure," I said, smiling. "But after I fix them up, nobody can tell."

"I guess only they can." Sabrina checked her reflection in the mirror, smudging her berry lip liner with her left pinkie. "And of course you."

We went to a bar on the edge of the city, near a highway overpass. Neon signs hung in the foggy windows. We played a couple games of pool and drank shots of cheap tequila. Every now and then Sabrina danced over to the old-school jukebox and flipped through the records, the light flickering over her face, her reflection a floating bust on the glass. I sat at the bar and watched a group of men circle around her. They held their beers close to their chests and waited for an opportunity to move in like vultures.

"We're going outside for a cigarette," Sabrina said.

Two pale-faced guys with broad shoulders and thick necks stood behind her, nervously casting glances my way, as if afraid I'd ruin their fun.

"But you don't smoke," I said.

"I picked it up," she said. "Just now."

I watched through the front window as she stepped outside and flopped against a parked minivan, twisting her hair around her fingers, her smile all teeth. The men stood next to her, packing their smokes. Neither was in her league. But Sabrina had a way of talking to men like she was a gift, an offering of an expressive pretty face and a girlish giggle. It didn't matter who it was, so long as they gave her attention back. After a while, I couldn't watch her anymore. I swiveled around on my stool and tried to catch the bartender's attention. He eventually came by, a white washcloth over his shoulder.

"That your sister?" he asked, glancing out the window.

"Not my sister." I looked at Sabrina tossing her hair back, the cords of her neck forming a chute to her collarbones. "My cousin."

"I knew you two were related." He poured tequila and set it before me. "You look similar."

"Not really," I said and swallowed my shot.

When Sabrina hobbled back inside, she could hardly stand in her wedged platforms. The men guided her by her wrists. She swayed between them until they released their grips and Sabrina leaned over me, her perfume gone rancid with hints of rotten fruit, something that belongs in the trash.

"Corina, Corina. Having fun?"

I glared at the two guys beside her. They were far less drunk than Sabrina and beaming with pride, as if they had already gotten her into a cab headed for one of their apartments.

"Let's get going," I said.

Sabrina squinted at me. Tiny wrinkles had begun to form around her eyes and lips. "You can leave me here," she said. "I'll get home okay."

With my hands firmly around her wrists, I towed her to the front door. The two men laughed, backed off, and began to circle around another girl a few stools down. The bartender pulled the white washcloth over the bar, eyeing the two of us while we left with what I thought was pity.

"Let's go." I was gripping Sabrina's wrist harder than necessary. She wobbled behind me and I squeezed tighter and angrier, worried my nails would mark her skin. "Don't you care how people look at you?"

Outside the air was cool, the moon surrounded by a thin cloud. I kept dragging Sabrina to the car as she tottered behind me, her face to the sky like that of a dreamy child. When I finally let her go, she steadied herself against my trunk, opening her blue eyes wide.

"They look at us the same way, Corina." She laughed and pointed to my face. "They look at us like we're nothing."

. . . . . .

I told her to get into the car and said she was drunk. As we drove home, I glanced at her worn-out face resting against the window and I felt something unknowable about Sabrina, some sadness at her core that moved between us like a sickness. Where did it come from? Or had it always been there, growing inside her, filling her lungs with its liquid weight. "Sabrina," I whispered, tapping her shoulder, but she was already asleep, and for the first time in my life, I missed someone sitting right beside me.

Sabrina's body lay on a chrome table surrounded by clear tubes and murky chemicals. Her head was propped up on a plastic stand. Her eyes were closed and her whitish mouth curdled along the edges. The room smelled of singed skin, disinfectant, and vinegar.

"These pretty girls." Carlos shook his head. "They get themselves into such ugly situations."

I stared at Sabrina, her dark hair framing the pale column of her rippled throat. The bruising spanned her entire neck. Bluish lines edged sour yellow and circled her indented vocal cords. Broken blood vessels spread to her collarbones. Her bloated chin was tilted stiffly to the right, perched oddly above it all.

"You think you'll be okay?" Carlos asked.

I exhaled, and hid my hands behind my back, my fingers lightly shaking. "I'll be fine. Where's the makeup?"

Carlos wheeled over a metal table. On it were several glass jars and brushes laid out in rows and a small cassette player–radio. "This makeup is different. It doesn't blend as well as your traditional products, but application is mostly the same. You know about the eyes and lips, right?"

"What about them?"

Carlos ran his hand above Sabrina's eyes. "We suture them shut to set them in an attractive pose. I used the picture you gave me. She should look like herself."

He handed me the photo from his pocket. Sabrina had taken it in my bathroom mirror. She was twenty-one, maybe twenty-two, at the time.

Carlos rubbed a freckle on Sabrina's forehead like he was polishing a piece of furniture. He turned on the radio. The Shirelles. A tune about a man doing all of us, every woman who had ever lived, wrong. Carlos told me to find him down the hall when I was done.

I walked around Sabrina's body. I reached out, touching her cheek, warmer than I had expected. I got to work, focusing on disguising the swelling of her temples and chin. Her right cheek had grown stiff with a ridge cutting near her lips. I filled it in with my thinnest brush and stepped back. Her lashes, I noticed, had grown longer in death. It almost made her look shy.

With a boar-bristle brush, I detangled her knotted strands. Her hair shone like spilled motor oil, greens and golds and blues all in that black. Corkscrewed sections bounced off my curling iron, more alive than anything else on that table.

For her neck, I grabbed a lime green concealer with olive undertones, a normal base coat for problematic rosacea. I dabbed a fanning synthetic brush into the jar and swirled it over my wrist. It was a good undercoat, even and heavy. Her throat felt plastic and ribbed where notches of hardened flesh had risen and stayed. They didn't give way as I worked the brush from her collarbones to her soft chin. I covered her skin in a solid flesh tone, a small pool of makeup congealing in the cup of her sternum. I used a tissue to wipe it away.

I considered checking the backside of her neck for bruising, but I realized that no one, not even my grandmother, would see.

. . . . . . . .

Sabrina was forever to face ceilings and casket tops padded in pink satin, and once she was lowered into her grave, her throat would collapse, slowly disintegrating into the dark.

By our mid-twenties, I saw Sabrina less and less. She worked nights. I worked days. She moved a few times and I lost track of her addresses, the names of her friends, the men she dated, the bars she tended. She rarely went to family dinners, but when she did, she was puffy-eyed and sallow-skinned, her slinky tops always falling off her shoulders. She'd gulp cups of black coffee like water, laughing at her own jokes, her hair swinging over my grandmother's table. After some time, we both stopped calling and, for a while, I thought she was fine with that.

At work one afternoon I was helping a white woman find blush. She was young and blond with a sheen to her skin that only comes from years of good nutrition, expensive moisturizers, and generations of tragedy-free living. I dusted shimmering golden rouge over her undefined cheekbones. She seemed pleased as she examined her reflection in a hand mirror.

"I always feel silly spending money on makeup," she said, handing me her Amex card.

"It's a good investment," I said, ringing her up. "Studies show that men find a woman's face to be her most sexually appealing feature, her body second."

From somewhere behind, I heard a coarse laugh. "That's a lie."

Sabrina stood at my counter in a short denim skirt with a misshapen purse slung over her shoulder, a neon-pink bra peeking out from her white tank top. She had parked herself beside the woman, who first gawked and then stepped quickly away, as though Sabrina was some escaped zoo animal. I did a quick scan of the sales floor, searching for my managers, but was relieved when none were in sight. Sarcastically, I asked Sabrina what she was doing there, so early, at noon.

"I miss you," she said, sweetly. "I thought tomorrow we could celebrate."

I gathered several kabuki brushes, positioning them on their base. "Celebrate what?"

"My birthday." Sabrina began spraying a bottle of Dolce & Gabbana's Light Blue down the front of her shirt. "I'm twenty-five tomorrow. We can shoot pool or cook dinner. Like old times."

I wanted to tell her that I was busy, but when I looked across the glass counter, her makeupless face shocked me. Her skin was as gray as old meat and her blue eyes were dull with crumbs of dried sleep in their corners. Her purse was stained, the zipper broken, the contents exposed—crumpled tissues, capless pens, two loose dollars. Sabrina, I decided, needed me.

"I'm off tomorrow at nine," I said. "Come over. We'll figure it out."

That night and the next day I kept thinking of Sabrina's filthy purse, its worthless contents. I made a run to the dollar store for decorations, white streamers and metallic glitter. I baked tres leches cake and wrapped presents—eye shadow, a tester bottle of Dior perfume, lipsticks. When everything looked like a wedding cake, all shiny and pastel, I sat on my bed and waited for Sabrina to arrive.

I had been asleep in the bluish light of my apartment when I woke up at midnight to someone banging on the door. Sabrina stood on the stoop, shivering in torn jeans and a hooded sweatshirt. She came inside, carrying the cold air on her body, taking a seat on my couch. Snowflakes melted in her black hair. "I walked here," she said. "You wouldn't believe how much it snowed. Everything is covered in white."

I knew she was drunk by the way she spoke. Her words weren't slurred, but softer than usual, almost angelic in their lightness.

"I kept thinking about that story," she said. "The one about the devil at the dance. Remember?"

My grandmother told the story often. A beautiful girl disobeys her family by sneaking into a midnight dance. She's only there for a short time when a good-looking man slinks toward her out of the crowd. She discovers he can dance well, and not just for an Anglo. He twirls her for hours until the girl notices the faces around her, wide-eyed and gape-mouthed. Her arms suddenly burn, then her lower back, and eventually her lips to throat—all the places where the man touched her. She screams as she notices that his feet, like the devil's, are hooved.

"It's funny the way Grandma tells it," Sabrina said. "When the girl notices a sour smell and it's her own flesh burning."

I told her it wasn't funny. I said it was horrible.

"You've always had a shitty sense of humor, Corina."

I handed over her presents. "Happy birthday, by the way. You're a day late. Where were you?"

Sabrina uncurled a smile, and with frenzied hands she unwrapped her gifts, shards of silver paper landing at her wet shoes. She pulled the items out one by one—blotting eye shadow over her wrists, running lipstick across her mouth, and spraying perfume along her throat. It was like watching a toddler at their birthday party, their eyes wide with amazement as they realize that every gift, every person, is there for them. "I went out," she said.

I paced between the front window and couch, the muted television the only light between us. "I waited for you all night. You could have called."

"I forgot."

"You asked me to see you. Not the other way around."

Sabrina stood from the couch and moved along the kitchen wall. She opened and closed cabinet doors, pushing herself taller on her tippy-toes, searching my shelves.

"I don't have any booze," I said.

She turned around, peering at me through the semidark, her eyes almost all white. "I'm looking for a water glass."

I grabbed one from the drying rack and thrust it into her hands. She rolled it between her palms, her fingernails jagged, their ruby polish chipped.

"What's wrong with you?" she asked. "Aren't we going out?"

I told her bars were closing soon. I said she was too late. Sabrina filled her glass with water and gulped it down in a few swallows. She wiped her mouth on the back of her sleeve, the water running over her chin. Her carelessness disgusted me. I wanted to throw the glass out of her hands and hold a mirror to her face, forcing her to see herself. "Can't you tell what people think of you? What I think of you?"

Sabrina smirked. "What does my little cousin Corina think of me?"

"You don't care," I said. "You don't care about anything, not even yourself. Look at the way you live."

Sabrina gazed toward me, her blue eyes vacant and glossy, as if she saw nothing. "So, how do I live? I mean, you would know. All you've done your entire life is follow me around."

"Pathetically," I said. "That's how."

She gathered her gifts from the couch, tossing them loudly into the trash. She put on her hood and secured the strings around her neck. "You're down here with the rest of us, Corina. You're just too ashamed to notice."

I turned to the window, where I saw myself streaked in light. "I'm nothing like you."

"You're right." Sabrina laughed. "I'm not some lonely makeup girl at the mall."

"You're a drunk," I said, my face burning with anger.

Sabrina opened the door, the snow falling white and golden behind her. "You've only ever had me," she said, stepping into the night. "Remember that when you have no one."

I watched through the window as she walked away, shrinking smaller in the distance, streetlights casting shadows around her in wide amber shafts. After some time, I stood outside on the stoop and breathed fog like smoke in her direction. By the time I thought of calling out her name, Sabrina was already down the block, too far to hear me, and too far to look back.


I took a seat in the last row of the viewing room. Classical music played from the ceiling speakers. Sabrina's casket was open, flowers arranged on either side, an ivory curtain behind it, making it look as though she was on a stage. Aunties and uncles walked with their arms linked. They gazed down, turned their heads to the side, whispered, and stepped away. Some of my cousins smoothed her hair. My mother kissed her hands. My grandmother snapped a photo as part of her normal routine at funerals. When it was my turn, I kneeled at Sabrina's casket and touched her face. It felt colder than before. There was lipstick on her forehead where someone had kissed her. I was smudging it away when my grandmother appeared at my side.

"Everyone is saying she looks beautiful, Corina." She petted my head and kissed my cheek.

. . . . . .

I thanked my grandmother and focused over her head at my family in folding chairs. They were arranged in rows with rosaries in their hands, their eyes swimming with muted colors. I looked at my youngest cousins, kicking their legs in white tights, pigtail braids, and red ribbons in their hair. I looked to my mother and father, dazed and accepting, numb to everything.

After some time, I heard my grandmother say to my auntie Josie, "It's what she would have wanted."

I thought of all the women my family had lost, the horrible things they'd witnessed, the acts they simply endured. Sabrina had become another face in a line of tragedies that stretched back generations. And soon, when the mood hit my grandmother just right, she'd sit at her kitchen table, a Styrofoam cup of lemonade in her warped hand, and she'd tell the story of Sabrina Cordova—how men loved her too much, how little she loved herself, how in the end it killed her. The stories always ended the same, only different girls died, and I didn't want to hear them anymore.

"No," I said, turning back to my grandmother before taking my seat. "Sabrina didn't want any of this. She wanted to be valuable."

Five months before the wake some girls from work invited me to a party on Colfax Avenue, in one of those stone mansions built by silver barons and their doe-eyed wives, a four-story house with a rounded balcony above a wraparound porch. Younger girls were huddled outside smoking cigarettes. They pulled deep drags and allowed the smoke to rise slowly from their heavily painted lips. One was telling a story about a guy she used to date who had recently been found stabbed to death in a dumpster. The other girls hung their heads until one of them cracked a joke. I stepped past them and went inside.

There were enough people crowded in the front room that the air was humid. A few unfamiliar faces were perched on the spiral staircase, sipping beers and drinking tequila from the bottle. It was dark save for a few dim lamps and a string of twinkling Christmas lights. In the hallway, I leaned against the wall and looked on at the kitchen, where people moved to an old doo-wop song. Women danced before their men. They lifted their hair, fanning their necks, their silver hoop earrings butting against their shoulders. That's when I saw someone break away from the dancing. She pushed through the crowd, heading for the hallway. When she stepped closer to me, I saw that it was Sabrina, skinny and wet with sweat. I hadn't seen her since her birthday.

She smiled with her blue eyes. "Where you been so long, Corina?"

On the porch Sabrina told me that she was moving to California, that she'd met a guy who was opening a bar, that she'd make tons of money. "You should visit me once I'm settled," she said.

I told her maybe I would. A black SUV pulled up outside the party. The headlights remained on and I could hear the dull thud of bass. Sabrina waved to the driver, who was hidden behind tinted windows. She threw her faux-leather jacket over her shoulders and hurried in stiletto boots down the porch steps. Halfway across the yard, she turned back. "What's your first memory in the entire world?"

"You know it's that time I got stung by a bee, but you claim it didn't happen to me."

"It doesn't matter," Sabrina said. "You can have that memory if you want."

She climbed into the black SUV, slamming the door behind her. As it pulled away, the window rolled down. Sabrina appeared from the shoulders up, shouting something I couldn't make out. It was winter's end. The road shimmered with black ice. All I could see was Sabrina's long hair coiling around her neck, pale as the moon.

# SISTERS

· · · · · · · · · · · · · · · · ·

... and the blind man looked up and said, "I can
see people, but they look like trees, walking."

MARK 8:24

In the weeks before Dolores "Doty" Lucero had her eyesight
stolen from her, she witnessed her life as if it were ordinary,
taking for granted the way sunlight pressed through lace curtains as she woke in the mornings. She didn't pay special attention to her younger sister, Tina, slumped on her side and snoring
loudly in her bedroom, one of her breasts slopping out of her
satin nightdress. She didn't stop to behold their familiar kitchen
with iron skillets drying on the rack and cracked eggshells in the
wastebasket. And outside, beyond their front windows, Doty
didn't consider the cottonwood trees and Sunshine elms on
their side of town, the Northside, along Federal Boulevard, a
neighborhood of duplexes and low bungalows.

On the morning the flyers appeared across the city like snow
in early July, Doty went outside to fetch the newspaper after
starting breakfast with Tina. She stepped out their duplex's
screen door with her hair crisp in black curls and her makeup
impeccable and bright. As she bent down to scoop up the Tues-

· · · · · · ·

day edition of the *Rocky Mountain News,* Doty caught sight of a misplaced whitish square. Walking barefoot over the grass, she stopped at the cottonwood tree, pulling a flyer down from the bark. The flyers were printed on cheap, brittle paper with a photograph of the girl, borrowed from the 1955 North High School yearbook, sitting dead center on the page. *Missing, Lucia Barrera, nineteen-year-old girl of Filipino descent works in leather goods at Montgomery Ward's, 16th Street and Tremont Street.*

Doty's chest ached with a hardened sadness. She lifted her gaze, eyeing the quiet street, almost hoping the missing girl would suddenly appear beside a mailbox or a parked automobile. Doty walked back inside through the sitting room, past the sofa, beneath the stucco archway, and into the kitchen, where Tina sat at the table with a plate of fried potatoes and flour tortillas piled before her. She was in her nightdress. Her hair was folded against her scalp with pins.

"This was on our tree," Doty said in Spanish, setting the flyer on the table and taking a seat.

Tina gave it a glance. She shrugged.

"You don't recognize her? She goes to Benny's and wears those fluttering cowgirl dresses. She goes to St. Catherine's, too, one of those Filipinas. You know, the girls who show up early for Mass and always bow lowest in the front pew."

Tina stared at her sister with dismissive and faraway eyes that sat deep in her face, surrounded by mounds of cheekbones and dark brows. She could be flippant, downright oblivious, but she was Doty's best friend and only family in Denver. Tina kindly looked at the flyer once more and told her sister that she'd never seen that girl in her life. "I don't really pay attention to the backs of heads at Mass," she said in English. "But I guess you do."

Doty swiped the flyer from the table and held it in the sunlight. She certainly knew the girl. She had first noticed her months earlier and often found herself watching her at church. Once, after Lucia had received communion, her head bowed and hands clasped in white gloves, she'd walked away from the priest and shocked Doty. Lucia had glanced in her direction, stuck out her pink tongue, and revealed the white wafer inside her mouth. She then smiled, disappearing back into her pew. Doty felt something like heat spread across the center of her dress. Lucia was very beautiful, with strong, precise eyes, and Doty felt an urge to know her.

Doty said, "I know you've seen her at church, Tina. What could have happened to her?"

"Maybe she's dead." Tina gulped a glass of orange juice. "Someone could have chopped her right up."

"Don't say something so ugly. That's horrible."

"Fine. She probably had a boyfriend," Tina suggested, her voice strained with annoyance. "I bet they ran off and wanted to get married in a hurry."

"I don't think so. She didn't seem interested in that."

Tina carried her dirty dish to the sink. She scraped the soggy remains of a half-eaten breakfast into the wastebasket while humming a country tune, her shoulder blades jutting from her back like stunted wings. "Come off it, Doty. Only you aren't interested in finding a man."

Doty said nothing. She reached for the flyer, running her fingernails down the missing girl's eyes as if putting her to sleep.


Tina and Doty had lived together for two years, since they left southern Colorado at sixteen and seventeen years old. Their mother had stayed in a town called Durango. She'd taken up with an older Anglo rancher named Weiss. In the beginning, he seemed a comfortable choice for their mother after her first husband drank himself to death. But Weiss began showing Tina and Doty attention neither wanted, hovering over their beds as they slept, placing his fat, callused palms across their cheeks as they dreamed. Though they pleaded with their mother to leave him, she was too broken inside. *What did they expect,* she had said. Weiss had a taste for pretty Indian and Spanish girls. As a parting gift, their mother gave the sisters twenty-seven dollars and some advice. "You girls get married sooner rather than later. You're good-looking enough."

The sisters found work downtown as receptionists for a hematologist. Doty had the morning shift, while Tina worked afternoons. Doty enjoyed the calm pace, the stack of new magazines, and the high-rise view of Civic Center Park. From her desk, she marveled at the gradual way the aspens, which grew in slim rows along the park, shifted their leaves. They went from green in summer to a color in autumn that resembled a thousand gold coins, flipped endlessly by an unseen hand. Tina tolerated the job because it held a special place in her heart. Four months earlier she had met her boyfriend, Randy, after he made a delivery on a Tuesday. That night over dinner, Doty was shocked at the certainty in her sister's voice when she said, "He will ask me to marry him someday. I know it." Doty meanwhile didn't plan on the servitude of marriage. She had no interest in men. She sometimes wondered if she'd get married at all.

That evening after the flyers appeared, Doty looked up from where she sat on the lime-colored sofa to see Tina walk in through the screen door. Her makeup had warmed in the summer heat, giving her face the look of a glazed doughnut.

. . . . . . .

"Get up," Tina said, jabbing her sister's leg. "We're going to the movies."

"It's Tuesday." Doty was already in her lounging clothes—cigarette pants and an old billowing blouse. "The Santa Fe isn't open on Tuesdays."

"We aren't going there. We're going to the other theater on a double date."

The other theater never played pictures in Spanish, and Doty suspected that, as usual, Tina had found her a date with a white man. Her sister had a thing for Anglos. They made more money, they could live and go anywhere in the city, and Tina believed each of the sisters could end up married to one. After all, they were both light-complected. But Doty felt white men treated her as something less than a full woman, a type of exotic object to display in their homes like a dead animal. The last time Tina had set her up, Doty endured a night out with an insurance man named Rustin Mitchel, who stank of sour mop water. At the end of the night, despite Doty shaking her head no, he moved in for a kiss. Doty leaned so far back that it became a game of limbo.

Tina said, "I ran into this guy outside the office fixing some trees for Dr. Marcus. His name is Joey Matthews. He's got a good job as an arborist or whatever you call it. He's real good-looking. Tall and, oh, Doty, he has these baby-blue eyes. You've never seen anything like it."

"Sure I have," Doty said. "Green eyes, blue eyes, black eyes. I've seen them all."

Tina pulled Doty up by both wrists from the couch. "You're going. End of it. And be nice this time. Maybe you'll know him the rest of your life."

Joey Matthews stood on the stoop and introduced himself with his cowboy hat dangling from his hands. He had milky skin the same color as his hair and perfectly square teeth. Above his thin upper lip, reddish seams from a scar, a harelip corrected, quivered as he spoke. He lowered his blue eyes, as though Doty's gaze could burn his face. "Pleasure," he said with a weak handshake, and then motioned for each of them—Tina, Randy, and Doty—to hop into his four-seater Ford pickup idling along the curb. Tina and Randy practically sat on each other's laps in the back. Up front, Doty pressed herself against the door as they drove away from the Northside, the sun setting, reflecting pink and gold over the rushing Platte.

Silhouetted against the low light, Joey turned to Doty, asking what sort of music she liked, his face cloaked in shadow. "Bet you like a lot of that Spanish junk," he said.

"No, not very much. I prefer Patsy Cline."

The ride was quiet after that.

At the drive-in, Joey parked with the truck's flatbed facing the screen. Everyone got in back on a thicket of woolen blankets. Doty carefully pulled herself up with one hand on her cotton dress, keeping her legs covered. The crowd was the usual Eastside variety, blond girls in expensive store-bought dresses and their boyfriends with big shiny cloud-colored Chevrolets. Doty could see a far-flung corner of the drive-in, the colored section, populated by friends from the Northside and Benny's dance hall, the area where she and Tina normally were seated. She found herself searching for Lucia's face. Maybe she had been found and was out enjoying the warm night at the movies. But Doty soon realized the colored section ended in a tall wooden fence, where several flyers for the missing girl had been posted. Lucia's pretty face was nowhere within the drive-in, and

Doty felt that same hardened sadness sinking from her throat to her stomach.

The last glimmers of dusk cooled behind the jagged mountains and the movie screen blasted with light. From the crackling speakers, circus music played while on-screen a cartoon hot dog danced with gloved hands and socked feet. The automobiles around them were hazy with cigarette smoke and mirrored lights. Doty felt anxious waiting for the picture to begin. She couldn't place the emotion's origins within herself, but she watched carefully as Joey breathed with his mouth slightly open, spit shining across his square teeth. Tina let out a piercing laugh from the other side of the truck bed. She looked like a little girl in a party dress, blue ruffles clear to her throat. She leaned into Randy, and threw her arms around his.

"Let's get a Coke, baby," she said, and they jumped off the truck, weaving between parking spots, her black hair and his felt hat bobbing between automobiles.

Joey slouched toward Doty; he smelled vaguely of soil. She scooted away. The movie's opening credits had started. A long black road rolled over the screen until the camera stopped on a platinum-blond actress in a torn black dress, her shoulders and hips exposed as she screamed, her hands sandwiching her pale face, her mouth open with dangly tonsils. Soon the camera cut behind her where ants the size of elephants with lasers for eyes descended upon the earth from an oval spaceship.

"Pretty night," Joey said.

"It's a night," said Doty.

Joey leaned back on his elbows and readjusted the blankets beneath them. Movie light poured over his face in changeable shades of white and gray. Doty caught herself staring at his scar, his knotted flesh. He covered it with his fist and went on.

"Listen," he said. "Have I done something to offend you?"

"No. Not at all." Doty pointed to the screen. "I'm just watching the picture."

"It seems a little ridiculous, don't you think?"

Doty laughed. Of course it was ridiculous. It was a movie with giant ants. "It's supposed to be. Funny, that is."

Tina and Randy returned with Cokes and small red bags of popcorn. They were arguing about something that had happened at the concessions stand. A young man Tina and Doty knew from the Northside had been thrown out of the theater for raising his voice when, after asking for a Coke, he was given a water. Tina wasn't upset it happened. She was going on about how it was normal. She couldn't understand how Randy never noticed.

"It's called getting the water treatment," Tina said, gripping the tailgate with one hand. "You've never heard of that, Randy? It happens to us all the time. You're at a nice Woolworth, and just like that the clerk closes her register when it's your turn. Or you're at some diner on Colfax and when you order a grilled cheese sandwich, the waitress comes back with an empty plate."

"Why would I notice that?" Randy asked, lowering his face to his hands and biting straight from the popcorn bag.

"Because you're a big tall American boy," said Tina, sarcastically.

Randy smirked. "And you're my little Spanish girl."

Tina smacked her lips and rolled her eyes. She then went to hoist herself onto the truck, but she slipped and fell backward, landing on the ground with a crack.

Doty sprang forward, peering over the truck's tailgate. "Don't just stand there," she said to Randy. "Help her!"

"Jesus, baby," he said, kneeling in the dirt at her side. "Are you okay?"

Tina threw her head back and let out a whimper. "It hurts so bad." She bent her left arm and showed everyone the blood pouring from her elbow, dripping into the dark soil. Randy handed Joey the concessions. He lifted Tina from the ground and slung her injured arm around his neck, getting blood on his collared shirt.

"She's a graceful one, your sister," Joey whispered to Doty and laughed.

Doty was shocked. She could laugh at Tina. She had laughed at her her whole life. But they were sisters.

"It's not like we're out dancing," Doty said, but her voice was muted by the movie's swelling music. The platinum-blond actress cried out in agony as the queen ant hoisted her from the earth. The sounds of flesh tearing filled the night as the image of a severed arm, dripping with blood, cascaded across the screen.

The next evening, Tina returned from work with a bouquet of lilies. They had yawning petals the color of sap. She placed them on the kitchen table, where Doty sat in a cotton blouse buttoned to her throat. Her fists were balled beneath her chin. In the corner, a new Patsy Cline album spun beneath a needle.

"Always this sad country stuff with you," Tina said, unzipping her work dress.

"Looks like someone got flowers for her boo-boo."

Tina was taking off her clothes, her mauve dress peeled from her shoulders and dangling around her waist like an extra layer of skin. She bent her arm, showing Doty the wound wrapped in gauze. A dark spot of blood seeped through the bandage. "Actually," she said, blowing on her elbow, "these aren't for me. They're for you. Joey sent them while I was at work. I guess he likes his women uptight and unaffectionate. Meanwhile, Randy doesn't so much as call to check on my arm. I mean, it could be broken. You saw how far I fell."

"You'll live," Doty said, petting the flowers. They were as soft and silken as a dog's ear. There was a note near the stems: *Something pretty for someone the same.* Doty withdrew her hand, as if it had been bitten. She felt an unfamiliar jolt below her ribs. She had never gotten flowers before. "Joey wasted too much money on these. I hope he doesn't expect anything in return."

"Why would he expect anything?" Tina slipped into her bedroom to change. She reappeared seconds later in a towel. "I forgot to tell you. They found that missing girl's jacket near the Platte River today. Right there beneath the bridge from the Northside to downtown. One of the patients at work was yapping on and on about it. 'What kind of world?' she kept saying. 'What kind of world?' "

"Her jacket?" Doty inhaled the lilies' sweet fragrance and felt like choking. She imagined a crumpled wool coat halfway submerged in river water, sooty and black. In her mind, she saw Lucia scrambling over the banks, scraping her knees and arms on rocks as the jacket was torn from her body.

Tina tucked her hair into an orange shower cap. "It's just awful. She's a dead girl now."

Doty lifted the flowers from the table. She set them beneath the large window near the sink. In the light, the petals appeared clear as screens. "Don't say that, Tina. She's not dead." Doty shook her head. "No, she can't be dead. She's probably just cold."

It was Saturday and Doty had reluctantly agreed to a second date. On the shores of a mountain lake called Dillon, a warm wind carried a fleck of sand into her left eye, blurring Doty's view of the water ablaze with ribbons of white. She recalled a bedtime story that her mother used to tell her and Tina about an evil water spirit roaming the Rockies. At night, when children are asleep, a white-haired man with pebbles for teeth steals their shadows, locking them in a mossy cabin on the lake floor. Doty rubbed her eyes and went to stand beside Joey as he unloaded an armful of fishing supplies from his truck.

A few feet from the shore, Joey spread a checkered blanket over the ground. He unknotted two fishing poles and jabbed live worms on their hooks. Doty sat down on the blanket and watched as he cast both their lines into the lake. Joey reeled the lines in a bit and nestled the poles within a crook in a small boulder. He then sat on the blanket and from a wicker basket pulled out cheese-and-jelly sandwiches, handing one to Doty, leaving dusty thumbprints along the crust. Doty slowly chewed her first bites as Joey asked her about her family. She explained that her mother was gone, her father dead, and that Tina was all she had.

Joey eyed her with an intensity reserved for judges and social workers. "It must be rough, being alone like that."

"Believe me," Doty said. "It's not."

Doty soon asked Joey about his job. He cut trees, this she knew, but Joey corrected her. It was much more complicated. He and his father planted seedlings, trimmed branches, studied bark. A new species of beetle, he explained, threatened to wipe out entire forests. He stood up, trekked over the rocks, and headed to the trees with wide, brisk strides. His boots crunched the ground as he went. Moments later, Joey returned with a black bug writhing between his index finger and thumb.

"They look like this," he said, "though this little guy isn't quite the same. Some people want to kill them, but I think even the ugly things deserve a chance to live. It's just about making sure things can live together without destroying each other."

"You should put that down," Doty said, peering into Joey's face. His expression was reserved, but his mouth showed a gleeful excitement, almost chaotic happiness. *Who said anyone deserves anything,* she thought, *especially some black bug?*

Joey laughed and blew the beetle out of his palm and it launched itself into flight over the lake. He sat down, closer to Doty than before. In the sunlight, his face almost seemed handsome apart from the babyish coloring of his cheeks and the pink line of his scar. He smelled even stronger of dirt than the last time. Doty leaned away. She caught herself fanning the air.

"What about you?" he asked. "You like that job with your sister? You two are secretaries, right?"

"Sure, it's fine." Doty searched for a smooth rock. She ran her palms over the ground until her eyes fell upon one that seemed polished somehow.

"You'd like to do that forever, as your career?"

Doty stood and walked the uneven earth toward the shore, her short heels jabbing into wet pebbles. She tossed the rock, dropping it into the water with a sonorous clop. "No," she said, looking back at Joey. His gaze was fixed on her face, as though it were as interesting to him as that flying beetle. "To be honest," she said with pride, "I'd like a more artistic job."

Doty searched the horizon and watched wisps of clouds collide. She went back to the blanket, easing down in her polka-dot sundress. "Maybe design shop windows," she said. "Sometimes I walk past those big department-store windows and I see all those beautiful dresses on the headless mannequins. It's awful. I could do a much better job. At the Montgomery Ward's, they had this big tulip dress hidden behind some beach ball. You could barely see what was important."

. . . . . . .

"That right?" Joey said.

Doty grew quiet. She thought of Lucia. She had once walked by Montgomery Ward's and, through the front windows, saw the girl laying out new pairs of leather gloves. She was bent over in such a way that Doty could see her neck, the place where her fine black baby hairs ended and the broad length of her back began. Lucia had turned around, and in an endearing bristle of movement, waved to Doty. She was too flustered to go inside and say hello. Now Doty wondered if she'd ever get the chance.

One of the fishing lines trembled, lightly ringing the bell at the top of the pole. Joey walked to the shore, where he methodically reeled in the smallest rainbow trout Doty had ever seen. "You shouldn't have to slave away all day at some office job or a lousy department store," Joey said over his shoulder.

Doty called out, "Excuse me?" She'd almost forgotten what they were discussing.

Joey pulled the fish from the hook, turned its slippery body over in his hands, and removed a knife from his trouser pocket. He slit the fish in a swift motion before deciding that it was too small for anything but waste. He tossed the dead fish into the lake and, without wiping his hands on a kerchief, sat back on the blanket, softly patting Doty's thigh, squeezing hard around her knee. He smelled strongly of the dead fish and Doty felt trapped, though the entire mountainside was open before her.

"You should be taken care of," Joey said. "A pretty girl like you deserves that."


"What's not to like?" Tina was lounging on the lime-colored sofa. The duplex was cool, smelling of juniper berries and flowery prefume. "He seems like a sweet guy. Plus he has that good job and doesn't look half bad."

Doty set two gin and tonics on the coffee table beside the magazines. She took a seat by her sister. "That's fine, but I don't feel right." She reached for her glass and sipped. "Something feels wrong."

"That," Tina said, reaching for her own glass, "isn't Joey's problem. You have some sort of hang-up. A personal problem. The only thing to help with that is—"

Doty tossed a throw pillow at her sister.

"I'm an injured woman," Tina screamed in feigned agony. "How dare you?"

"How dare you harm me by setting me up with these ridiculous men?"

"Good," Tina said. "Glad you feel that way. Because we're going out to Benny's tonight. You, me, Randy, and Joey."

"I was just with him yesterday. I don't need to see him again tonight."

Tina set down her glass loudly. She sat with perfect posture and sighed, gently moving Doty's bangs away from her eyes with both hands. "Listen, I know you think we can afford to live in this duplex forever, but we can't. You need to find yourself someone, and what you do in your own time, away from him, well, that's your business."

Doty turned to the window. The sheer curtains rose and fell, splintering the sunlight along the hardwood floor. She thought of telling Tina that she wouldn't go—that she'd stay home and read, fix her hair, anything—but when she opened her mouth, she felt her hands tilting the drink down her throat instead.

Benny's sat on a tree-lined avenue beneath the burn of several evenly spaced streetlamps, a rotund building with an elongated entrance and wooden Spanish doors. Inside, the waxed floor reflected the thousands of tiny lights strung up between the buttresses and corner walls. Circular tables were draped in lace cloths, tinted lamps illuminated the bar, and Northside and Westside men and women in their finest clothes grouped themselves in fours or fives along the walls.

Doty slumped at a table with Joey, her arms folded in the lap of her peach gown. They had driven separately from Tina and Randy, who energetically danced in the center of the floor. When Doty and Tina first started going to Benny's, they always arrived and left together. They mostly sat at the tables along the front, Tina scoping out the room for the best-looking men and the prettiest girls. "Competition," she always said, but Doty never cared for the men there, and she didn't view the women as competition. She simply enjoyed them, their beautiful clothes and hair, their bright happy faces.

"We should dance." Joey reached across the table for Doty's wrist.

She stared at the edge of the hall. A band wailed onstage. The musicians lowered their trumpets. Halos of light bounced off their brass and fell onto the dancing couples, Tina and Randy among them, in a sea of bopping heads and swaying hips. Joey stood and placed his hands on Doty's shoulders. "Come on," he said. "You can teach me how it's done."

Joey led them between the waving bodies until a wall of dancers surrounded them. He pulled Doty close, his right arm resting on her lower back, his left hand cupping her right palm. His skin was warm and moist and soft as a child's. Doty tried to distance herself, but Joey held her torso to his, near enough that his chin was a sharp line edging over her curls. Doty moved as little as possible, finding herself bewildered by the other dancers and their enthusiasm. When she felt Joey's arms tipping her into a spin, she cemented her heels to the floor and said, "I'm no good at those."

"Sure, you are," he said and flung her body outward. Doty wobbled, her back knocking against a couple. Joey pulled her in once more and then released her with such force that this time she twirled, watching the blurring sight of naked shoulders, pearl necklaces, exposed teeth, closed eyes. Doty raveled back into Joey's arms, turning to look over her shoulder. Tina and Randy had returned to the table. Doty yanked herself away from Joey, and he followed as she hurried to her sister.

Both Tina and Randy were drunk, swaying a little to the left in their seats, laughing obnoxiously and giving one another sloppy kisses. Beneath the table, Randy passed a metal flask filled with whiskey to Doty. She leaned down and took a swig, then another and another. It seemed if she could get drunk, the night would be more bearable.

Tina stood and leaned forward over the table, her cleavage spilling from her neckline. She pulled a tube of cinnamon lipstick from her beaded clutch and offered it to Doty. "Here," she said. "Looks like you could use a touch-up."

Doty reached for the lipstick but stopped when she noticed Tina's left hand. A small golden ring, a single diamond, glistening like a tear. She looked at Tina's face, found her eyes. "Is that an engagement ring?"

Tina eagerly nodded before squealing out a yes.

"Yee-haw, Randy," Joey said, shaking his hand in congratulations.

Tina inched back and kissed Randy on the neck. "Well, aren't you happy for us?"

Doty forced a smile. She stood and hugged her sister. "Of course I am."

. . . . . . .

On stage, the music quieted and an older Filipina woman in a white dress and matching hat walked beneath the lights, clasping a photograph. The crowd clinked glasses and yelled over one another, uncoordinated as they danced without music. Tina still held her left hand in the air, awkwardly displaying her ring as the faces around her moved their attention to the stage.

"I have an announcement," the older woman said into the microphone.

"Oh God," said Tina, melodramatically. "This isn't the place."

"My daughter is missing," said the woman on stage. "Her name is Lucia Barrera—"

Tina waved to the table behind her, showing off her ring to a group of girls eating cake. "It's just gorgeous!" they hollered and Tina agreed with a high-pitched yelp.

"Can you just shut up?" Doty screamed at Tina.

"My goodness," Tina whispered, her expression oddly flat. "You can't be happy for your own sister getting engaged. What's wrong with you, Doty?"

"I don't care about your stupid ring. A girl from our own neighborhood is missing." Doty felt her pulse in her lips and her tongue prickled, as though it had fallen asleep. For a moment, she felt bad that she had spoken so harshly.

Tina's face had lost its gloating sheen and had been replaced with an angry, snarled expression. Then, as if she had told herself a joke in her head, Tina drunkenly laughed in Doty's face. "Oh, were you in love with that girl? Are you an invertida or something?"

Doty pulled away from Tina with disbelief and held her own cheek with one hand, as if she had been slapped. She studied her sister's face, her eyelashes fluttering like dusty drapes and her bottom lip turned inward until Doty saw only teeth. "Why would you say something like that?"

"Relax, Doty," said Tina, rolling her eyes. "It's just a joke."

Joey and Randy were laughing now. They both told Tina to stop, that she was drunk and might say something else she'd regret. The woman onstage finished her plea as the band quietly rumbled into a new set. All around them the dull thud of music vibrated the room. Doty got up from the table and turned to Joey as he impatiently chewed a plastic straw.

"Do you mind if we get going?" she asked. "I've got the worst headache."

Joey drove with the windows down, the night wind rushing against their faces. He fumbled with the radio until he found a station. The song was sullen and crackled. Slow country. The way Doty liked it. Joey drove the back way to Doty's duplex, easing into his stops and remaining still for far longer than necessary. She watched as he purposefully missed the turn for her street. She slouched down and held her hand to her forehead. *How typical,* she thought, rubbing her closed eyes.

He pulled into a dirt lot overlooking the city, an industrial area not far from her neighborhood, and backed up to the edge. Abandoned cars and enormous rusted machinery littered the ground. Joey shut off the engine. The music faded with the headlights.

"I live the other way," Doty said.

Joey stepped out of the truck. He came around to Doty's window. "I know," he said, "but you gotta see this."

Doty reluctantly opened her door. Joey led her behind the truck. They crawled onto the flatbed. In the distance, there were newly constructed high-rises, old stout brick complexes, and the constant blaze of the Olinger Mortuary sign illuminating the hillside like some advertisement for a 24-hour diner.

. . . . . . . .

"See those trees over there?" Joey pointed toward an umbrella of leaves in the distance. "My pops and me planted those years ago. He took me as a kid. I must have been five or six. It's strange. I feel like they're mine, in a way."

"How sweet," Doty said. She could feel Joey's eyes on her face, and then his palm beneath the pleats of her peach dress. She looked at the mound of his fist beneath the fabric, wondering how long she could let it stay there without feeling like toxic sludge was burning her skin. Not very long. "Don't do that," she said.

Joey put his hands in the air, as though he'd been caught stealing candy from a jar. He tilted away from her. "Did what your sister said bother you? You wanted to get out of Benny's quick."

She sat staring beneath her feet at the gravel, an ocean of dirt, swirling and rising and swelling below her shoes. "I wouldn't say I'm too happy right now."

Joey leaned toward her again. He had a rough patch of mousy stubble. It stabbed out of his chin, circling his mouth, the area of his scar bald. He moved closer and casually, as if they were in a movie theater, slipped his right arm over Doty's shoulder. "You're upset she said those things?" His fingers tapped her collarbone. "Don't worry. You can prove her wrong."

Joey placed his hand on the back of Doty's neck. He kept it there even after she threw her face forward, her hair coming around her eyes like blinders on a horse.

"I'm tired and want to go home," she said, searching the ground for a large rock.

"Your sister will be gone soon, and how will you afford that duplex by yourself? What're you planning to do? Get some nothing job putting dresses together in windows? You can't live like that."

Doty hopped down to the gravel. She stood very still with her hands on her hips.

Joey sat back with his legs crossed. "I wasn't trying to offend you," he said. "It's just, you're a beautiful girl. If you let someone help you, they will. Do you understand what I'm saying?"

"I don't give a damn what you're saying," Doty said. "And I don't need help. Take me home right now, and if you don't, I'll walk."

Joey uncrossed his legs. He swiped his hands through his milky hair, pulled a deep breath, and stepped off the truck. He walked toward Doty, getting as close as he had when they were dancing. He grabbed her arm, squeezing it until she knew, in the morning, there'd be a bruise. "It's not safe to be out alone. At this hour. In this spic neighborhood."

"I'm perfectly fine," Doty said, trying to pull her arm out of his grip. "I live in this neighborhood."

"Fine," Joey said, releasing his hold. "But why can't you just give me a kiss?"

Doty began to run. She cut between car parts and broken tools, a slab of metal siding, an empty paint bucket, and a few loose shoes. The sights of the city smeared together into one string of bluish light. Suddenly she felt Joey's hand clamp onto her wrist. He came at her with the force of a rabid dog gnashing into her flesh. Doty struggled to rip her body away, screaming, her voice echoing across the hillside.

"What're you doing?" Joey asked. "Stop this."

But Doty didn't stop. She kicked and squirmed, and realized the entire weight of her body dangled from Joey's arms. When it was clear that he would not let go unless she went back to the truck, Doty gathered wind in her lungs and screamed into Joey's face. Against her voice, he held his neck straight, the long bulb of his Adam's apple falling with a swallow. Doty sucked in another breath until her lungs ballooned with the night. She opened her mouth, releasing a cry, but Joey reached up and muzzled her face like an animal. "You shut up," he said, throwing her backward.

Doty landed belly-down, her head loudly splitting against a severed car door. She reached up to her right temple and felt her hair wet and warm like a swamp. Doty waved her hands before her face, but in the space between her eyes and the world, there was only darkness. She felt the unmistakable liquid warmth of blood leaking into her eyes, stinging all the way into her mouth. She sifted her fingers through rocks and broken glass, telling herself to see something, anything. "I can't see," she frantically screamed. "I can't see."

Doty quieted as weakness overcame her body. She listened to her labored breaths and Joey's boots crunching gravel before she felt the familiar tug of his arms lifting her from the hillside and carrying her body into his truck. She heard Joey's truck sputtering to life, and the radio, low like it played inside a tin can. They glided over what Doty suspected was Thirty-third Avenue, a street more desolate than the main road. Joey stopped the truck at maybe a red light, and Doty could feel blood on her palms and smeared across the vinyl seat.

"You're not very bright," he said, the soil smell coming from his mouth. "Drinking so much you fell."

"I can't," said Doty with great difficulty. "I can't see."

"Lucky for you I was there. Just the two of us, and I saved you."

Doty faded out of consciousness just before she felt the familiar curve of the park where she walked each morning under the coolness of the aspen trees.

—

As quickly as the flyers came, they fell from the cottonwood trees and Sunshine elms. They littered lawns and gathered in gutters. Old men crept out from their houses and hosed them away. Lucia Barrera's face flowed down streams and into the sewers, where it disintegrated into nothing more than ink-laced dust. In time, her face was forgotten, leaving the bark as naked and twisted as it had ever been. But then came an unusually warm morning in mid-September, when the faces of women rushing about the neighborhood on their way to work were slick with sweat and melted cosmetics. Many of them stopped, blotted their faces dry with silk handkerchiefs, and widened their coal-lined eyes as they received the news that Lucia Barrera, like most missing things, had been found. A mailman had spotted her north of the city, exiting a highway diner with glass doors. The *Rocky Mountain News* printed a photo of Lucia flanked by her parents, her shoulders bent inward, her chin tilted down.

"Isn't there more to the story?" Doty asked Tina over breakfast.

Tina shook out the paper. "Of course, but no one's saying a word."

Doty leaned over her plate of fried potatoes. "How does her face seem?"

"Relieved, I'd say. God only knows what she went through."

For a moment, Doty allowed her mind to wander. "God only knows."

On Tina's wedding day, nearly nine months after Lucia had been found alive, Doty sat on the toilet's closed lid, twisting a tube of coral lipstick between her hands.

"A little much on your bottom lip." Tina looked on, propped

against the doorframe in her wedding dress. Her gardenia perfume mixed oddly with the odor of mold as she passed behind her sister, tearing a piece of toilet paper from the roll. She worked Doty's face as if it were a fogged windshield.

It was many hours into the reception when a girl with an easy, somewhat deep voice asked Doty if she'd like a drink. She took a seat at her round table near the edge of the church's grassy courtyard. It was dusk, and the air was turning sharp, bitter. The girl sounded familiar, and the unseen parts of her, her voice and perfume, were musical and sweet in the way they collided. One gin and tonic turned into three and soon the girl blurted out an apology before asking Doty what happened to her eyes (it wasn't that they were ugly, just turned every which way). The other guests had moved onto the dance floor. Doty could feel white streamers blow over the grass, their own kind of shadows.

"I had an accident."

"Oh, no," said the girl, scooting closer to Doty and squeezing her hand. "I bet people say you're lucky it wasn't worse."

"As a matter of fact," said Doty, "no one says anything about it at all."

# REMEDIES

. . . . . . . . . . . . . . . .

A dermatologist with a can of liquid nitrogen can remove a wart in four to five seconds. I can remove one overnight with a clove of garlic and a Band-Aid. Your fingers will stink for days, but the wart will never come back. You won't have to bite or scratch at it until blood rushes over the spongy lining. You can hold someone's hand without shame or embarrassment.

I learned how to do this from my great-grandmother Estrella. She taught me all the remedies she learned from her own grandma on their pueblo in northern New Mexico. If you have a stomachache, drink chamomile tea with honey at the hottest temperature possible without scalding your tongue. If you have a headache, put slices of potato at your temples and let them draw out the pain. If you have a cold or a broken heart, drink a warm cup of atole made only with blue corn.

———

Our lice came from Harrison, though Mama didn't realize it was him the first time. She just tried washing my hair with mayonnaise. She heard about this trick from another hygienist at the dentist's office and came home with a big jar of Kraft, the good stuff. She held my head over the kitchen sink, took a serving spoon, and plopped hunks of mayo across my scalp. With a Marlboro Light bumping up and down on her lip, she swirled the mess into my long brown hair until my entire head was soppy and warm. As she puffed smoke in and out of her lipstick mouth, I could see the missing tooth on her right side, the spot she always hid from everyone, including me. After she finished, she put a plastic bag over my hair, tying it at the middle of my neck with a rubber band.

"Here," she said, pointing with her red nails to a chair at the kitchen table. "Sit for fifteen minutes, jita."

She dashed out her cigarette on a saucer and parted her own dark hair, leaning over the countertop and examining her pale scalp with a teal Cover Girl compact mirror. Her gaze went up and down and back again. Mama then snapped shut the compact and looked at me.

"All right, baby girl. Put your head over the sink."

With my face dropped into the sink's chrome basin, Mama rinsed my hair as her large breasts pressed into my back. Hot water spilled over the front of my Tweety Bird T-shirt, soaking my neck and chest. I whined, fighting back nausea from the egg-smell of my own head.

"Mama," I said. "Why can't we just ask Grandma Estrella about lice?"

"Look at me." She turned my body around and dried the water from my face with the bottom of her T-shirt. "You can never tell your grandma Estrella you have lice."

I tried to ask her why, but Mama shoved my head back under the faucet and kneaded my hair with her strong hands the way I had seen Grandma Estrella knead masa on Christmas Eve. As my brown hair wetly twisted, water rushed into my eyes, blurring my vision, but I swore I saw white lice eggs against the drain's black pit.

It was snowing the first time we picked up Harrison. Mama drove us to an apartment on Grant Street in downtown Denver and we huddled in our scarves and secondhand Sorels beneath the red-tarp awning at the front entrance.

Mama pushed a button on the intercom and a sleepy voice answered, "Who is it?"

"It's us," she said. "Millie and Clarisa."

A quick buzz vibrated the brass speaker box and Mama pulled on the lobby's door handle. Before we stepped inside, she hesitated, looking down at me.

"Now, this is your brother," Mama said quietly. "I know you haven't met him and I know that we never see Daddy anymore, but Harrison isn't as fortunate as you are, so be kind to him."

After I promised to be nice, we went inside, where the carpets were puke green and the ceiling was made of tin. We walked up a flight of creaking stairs while competing smells of garlic and mildew followed us. At the end of the second-floor hallway, Mama knocked hard on 13B.

Harrison's mom answered the door. She wore an enormous pink sweatshirt with the neck cut away, showing a star tattoo on her upper left shoulder. Her thin blond hair was pulled high on her head in a sloppy bun, and when she smiled, her teeth were very crooked.

"Oh, hi," she said. "Harrison, come here, Son."

He appeared next to her, hunched over and skinny, looking downward at the floorboards.

"Have fun with your sister," his mom said in her drowsy voice before handing him a backpack. She leaned over and kissed Harrison on the forehead. Behind her, I could see some of their apartment, a dusty living room with a sagging brown couch covered in laundry. There were pairs of crinkled and silky underpants beneath a grimy glass coffee table.

Harrison's mom rubbed her eyes with both hands, smearing her makeup until a speck of mascara floated inside her left eye. "He never said you were such a nice lady." She then blew a kiss to her son before closing the apartment door.

Mama flashed a warm smile. "Do you remember me? I met you when I came over to talk to your mom. You're going to stay with us for a couple days."

Harrison nodded and scratched his head. "You brought Tootsie Rolls."

"Gross. That candy sucks," I whispered.

Mama jabbed the back of my neck with her long red nails. "This is Clarisa. She's your half sister. You guys are almost the same age."

"You're ten?" Harrison asked.

"No," I said. "I'm eleven. I'm short for my age."

"I'm not," he said. "My mom says I get that from my dad."

The three of us started down the hallway, and I was surprised when we walked past a bathroom built into the wall, like a lime-green coat closet. I peered inside at an old porcelain bathtub with claws at the bottom. Grandma Estrella had a tub like that in her upstairs bathroom. I asked Mama about it and she told me that in the old days people shared bathtubs. They shared everything, she explained. But later when I asked Grandma

Estrella, she told me those hallway bathrooms were only in buildings where dirty people lived, people who did awful things for a living, people she prayed for each night before she rubbed cold cream on her face in slow upward strokes, because downward caused wrinkles.

Grandma Estrella lived in a red-brick Victorian house on the edge of a park named Benedict. She was a short, wide woman who wore long colorful skirts and carried on her skin the scent of rose oil and Airspun face powder. She lived alone, since my great-grandpa passed away before I was born and their only daughter died in a car crash when Mama was just four years old. Mama and I lived with Grandma Estrella after Daddy left, and even after we got our own townhouse in Northglenn, we visited her every weekend—except when Harrison came over. Mama said it was because we were busy, but I knew the truth. While Grandma Estrella hated all of Harrison, she only felt that way about half of me, my father's half, the white half.

One weekend, while I was staying over Grandma Estrella's, we baked cookies she called biscochitos. We were in her big kitchen with all the windows open, the yellow curtains rising and falling with a breeze. We watched *Bewitched* on the countertop TV, and when the episode ended, *Jerry Springer* came on.

"Ah, mija, I hate watching these hillbilly white people," Grandma Estrella said. "Look at this man." She was using a large wooden roller to point at the TV. "He was given every chance to make it in this world and what did he do? Threw it away on booze and drugs and can't take care of his family. Just like your father."

"I guess," I said, licking my spoonful of raw cookie dough.

"Him leaving your life was the best thing that ever happened to you and your mother. If he wouldn't have left on his own, I would have chased him off myself."

I laughed. "You'd chase him, Grandma Estrella? With what?"

"A broom, or maybe a coat hanger. There are many tools. Now, my baby, switch the station. I want to watch my stories."

I wiped my flour-covered hands on the white-lace apron she had made especially for me and clicked the dial to channel seven. The picture was soft on purpose, part of the show. White people with diamonds and pretty eyelashes kissed or lied and cheated on each other. That's how Grandma Estrella liked her people on TV—rich and scandalous.

Grandma Estrella said, "Doesn't Tiffany look gorgeous this week? Why don't you grow your hair like that, mija? A girl's hair should always be long."

I looked at the ends of my brown hair. "It quits growing after my shoulders."

"Nonsense. I know some herbs you can make into a tea."

Grandma Estrella closed her tiny eyes behind her large glasses and silently moved her lips as if she were reading different scraps of paper in her mind. After some time, she opened her mouth, the ridges in her face spreading wide and smoothing over, making her appear young again, if only for a second.

"I'll tell you the recipe for long hair, mija, but you must be cautious with this tea."

"Cautious?" I asked.

"Vanity is risky, my baby. Let me tell you, you had a great-great-aunt, Milagros, the same Milagros your mother is named after, and she used the herbs too often and her black hair grew so long and so beautiful that all the men in our pueblo and even from far away wanted to marry her, but she would not choose one because she believed the longer and more beautiful her hair grew, the better her choices of husbands would be until one night, when the rest of the children were sleeping soundly in the same bedroom, her hair coiled around her neck like a snake, squeezing all the life from her throat."

"That really happened?"

"Of course! You're calling me a liar?"

I pushed my dough scraps into the wastebasket and wondered what my own hair was capable of.

Whenever Harrison stayed over, Mama pulled out the extra comforter, the one with holes and all the cotton bunched together in the corners. She'd spread it over the couch, making up a little bedroom for him, where they'd sit for hours, watching movies and laughing. Mama often asked Harrison questions, and they were usually about our dad.

"Does Daddy ever send you presents?"

"One time he did. A Hot Wheels set."

"Oh, wow," Mama said, reaching out and stroking his neck. "What about your mama? Does he send her money to help out?"

"I don't know. Maybe."

"I hope so. He can afford it. You know, Harrison," she added with a sincere smile, "you look so much like Daddy. It's like you're him but as a little boy."

Each time I walked into the living room, I looked at Harrison's slumped-over body on the couch and felt something like hot blacktop tar in my guts. I hated to be around him. I didn't care that Mama said I should feel sorry for him because our dad was long gone and his mom had problems with drinking and taking pills. *Imagine if I slept all day,* Mama told me. *You'd never get a warm meal.*

. . . . . . .

With Harrison in our living room, the whole townhouse smelled as bad as his apartment building. He had dark bags under his eyes, like someone hit him real hard and never let him heal. His T-shirts had holes in the sleeves and his jeans were worn thin, covered in a fine layer of dirt at the butt and knees. The worst part, he smelled like pee.

"Hey, Harrison, why don't you use that bathtub in the hallway at your crappy apartment?"

"No one uses that, Clarisa. It's busted and old."

"You probably should. You smell like a litter box."

"No, I don't. I took a shower today!"

"Why does my mom have to take care of you, anyway? What's wrong with your own mom?"

"Nothing. She's just my mom."

Harrison never had a comeback and he never told on me for being mean. Instead, he acted crazy. In the middle of the afternoon, he'd open my dresser drawers, stick his face against my T-shirts and jeans, turn on and off our microwave, and ask annoying questions that made me wonder what his life was like at home.

"Do you get recess even when it snows real bad?"

"No, we have an inside day."

"How about your teacher—is she nice? What color is her hair?"

"For your information, my teacher is a guy."

"A guy, really?"

"Leave me alone. Don't you go to school, too?"

"What about our dad? Why doesn't he want to see any of us?"

"Maybe he doesn't want lice."

He was only a year younger, but even then I knew we were worlds apart. What I hated most about Harrison—besides that each time he came over, the lice came back—was that my mother was right. He looked like my dad. Even as a little boy, he looked like Daddy.

I was nine years old the last time we spent Christmas with Daddy. He was up unusually early, no black bags under his eyes or sour breath reeking of beer and cigarettes. He was happy, smiling and kissing Mama on the mouth. We played airplane and he whirled me around his one-bedroom apartment, giggling and cheering, my arms open like little wings. Mama cooked all day—ham, cranberry sauce, green bean casserole, cornbread. No Christmas tamales like at Grandma Estrella's, though. He never liked that.

We were together, sitting at his fold-out card table in the corner of the living room, when Daddy started the prayer. I gazed at the creases around his dark eyes, wondering if I would get those someday. I loved being near him when I could—loved it when he cupped his hand on the back of my neck and I could feel his calluses coarse against my skin. He reminded me of work, of cars, that special orange soap he used to wash away grease.

"Millie," he said. "You forgot the butter, honey."

Mama glanced at me and asked if I would be nice enough to get Daddy some butter. I hopped out of my chair and headed for the tiny kitchen. I walked by the overflowing garbage, where a sparkling green Christmas card was shoved beneath empty green bean cans and cracked eggshells. I don't know why I did it, but I stuck my hand inside the trash, pulling out the mushy card. When I opened it, a picture fell out of a little boy with dark eyes and light brown hair swinging a baseball bat. I stared into his face for a long time.

"Clarisa," Mama yelled from the table. "Did you find it?"

I shoved the Christmas card as far as I could back into the garbage. I grabbed the butter for the table and told my parents that I would be right back—that I needed to wash my hands before dinner.

In Social Studies, I scratched and scratched until a louse slid down the back of my neck and onto Chantel Sanchez's desk. She screamed so loud that the principal heard it from his office, or that's what the other kids claimed. It was the fourth time in a year that I had gotten lice from Harrison. I was sent home from school, indefinitely, until the issue was resolved. "Expelled due to health hazards" is what the official pink slip read. Mama was more upset than usual about the lice. She tried mayonnaise, then olive oil, then rubbing alcohol, then over-the-counter shampoos. By the time she had finished, I thought I would never go back to school.

The next Saturday, Mama took Harrison and me to a hair salon in a part of town called Wash Park. The salon was painted blue and white with mirrors in every direction. Techno music came out of the ceiling speakers and the floor was lightly scented with ammonia. The hairdressers were vibrant with colorful hair and face piercings. They had names like Celeste, Luna, and Sky. I flipped through a booklet with different hairstyles, showing Mama cuts I thought she might like.

"Look at her bangs," I said, folding the page over for Mama to see.

"Those are nice, jita. You guys are also getting haircuts."

"Here?" Harrison looked up from his seat, a surprised expression on his face.

"Yup. Don't need to worry about picking out anything new. I told the ladies what to do."

My hair had recently grown extra-long with the help of Grandma Estrella's tea. Mama normally took me to Cost Cutters for a trim, but last time, we were refused service. No one gave a reason why, but I knew it must have been lice.

When a woman called my name, I jumped out of my seat and I stuck out my tongue to Harrison. He ignored me, scratching his head. Then another lady called his name. They brought us to a row of black spinning chairs, seating us side by side. My hairdresser snapped peppermint gum in her mouth. She had glitter across her eyelids and her teeth were the whitest and biggest I had ever seen, like those white ladies in Grandma Estrella's stories. After she parted my hair with a black comb, she pointed beside me to Harrison, draped in a purple cape.

"Are you guys twins?" she asked. "What do they call that, paternal?"

"No," said the lady cutting Harrison's hair. "It's fraternal."

"That's it," my hairdresser said. "You sure do look about the same age."

Harrison giggled. "I wish we were twins. That'd be cool."

"He's just my half brother," I said.

The hairdressers shared a knowing look and I glanced away, toward the front windows.

Outside, seagulls dived between streetlamps. The sun was going down and the whole neighborhood was a shadowy pink. A family carrying pizza boxes walked together through the parking lot. It was a mom, a dad, and three little boys. The mom was laughing, pointing at her husband, who had grabbed a shopping cart and was riding the back like a scooter. His sons tried copying him. They wobbled everywhere, and the mom seemed worried. For just a second, I felt jealous of that family, their happiness and togetherness. Maybe if I had always known

Harrison, we could have been friends. But instead, he reminded me of Daddy, the only person who had ever left me. The family then walked out of sight and I looked back at the mirror.

That's when I burst into tears.

My long hair was gone, gathered across the floor like piles of dust. The hairdresser kept asking what was wrong, but all I could do was clutch my short hair, wetter in the front from all my tears.

"Don't cry, Clarisa," I heard Harrison say. He was whimpering quietly. His head had been shaved completely bald.

I stood up then and looked for Mama. She was behind us at another station, her expression downturned and sorrowful. Her long black hair had been trimmed into a spiky undercut with short bangs. When her eyes met mine, she mouthed something, maybe *sorry*.

On our way out, Mama handed the receptionist a check and one of the women tried selling her an antidandruff shampoo.

"You know, the kids both have it pretty bad," the woman insisted. "This will help for sure."

Mama shook her head, her short hair stationary against her scalp. "Thanks, but we'll try some home remedies first."


Mama was crying. Harrison and I heard her when we were fighting over whose turn it was for the only working Nintendo controller. At first it sounded like the neighbor's dog yipping, but it grew louder and steadier. I threw down the controller and Harrison followed me. Sitting on the toilet with the lid closed, her head in her hands, Mama was itching and pulling at her short hair, red bumps all over her scalp and neck. Snot and tears dripped down her face, over her lips, and onto the front of her white shirt. I stood in the doorframe, afraid to go near her. I had only seen her like this one other time—when Daddy left for good.

"They won't go away." She sobbed into her hands, gargling a bit.

"What, Mama?"

"They just won't go away."

Harrison stood behind me, his dark eyes filling with tears that lingered above his bottom lashes. I could see the bathroom reflected in his eyes—Mama, alone, on the toilet with hair in her lap and across the floor. I wanted to scream at him to leave, to walk home, take a bus, find some way to get out of our lives, but instead I just told him to watch Mama while I ran to the kitchen and did what I was never supposed to do—I called Grandma Estrella.

I told her what happened, and had been happening for months. She screamed so loud that when she finished, I heard true silence in our townhouse kitchen. Dust sifted through shoots of sunlight. Water dripped from the chrome faucet. The phone's cord slowly rolled. Everything was calm until Mama's sobs bumped throughout the hallway, interrupting the dead air. She didn't hit me or scream at me when I told her Grandma Estrella was expecting us. Mama got up from the toilet lid, silent and red-faced, and walked to the car, as if she had been expecting this day from the beginning.

When we arrived, Grandma Estrella stood on her porch, one hand over her eyes, scanning the yard with a watchful, hawklike gaze. She wore a wavering purple skirt, the brick house like a castle behind her. Mama parked and got out of her car, flicking a cigarette into the road as she walked us to the porch.

"Look at your hair," Grandma Estrella said. "Every one of you."

"It'll grow back," Mama said, quickly wiping tears from her face.

Grandma Estrella grunted some. She stepped aside and motioned with both hands for us to follow her. Before she opened the front door, she reached out to Harrison's small hand and introduced herself as Mrs. Lopez. Harrison's dark eyes grew wide and seemed to fill with wonder. It was like he didn't have grandparents of his own, and I realized he probably didn't.

"All of you, upstairs."

We climbed the cherry-oak staircase to the upstairs bathroom. The long white porcelain basin of the claw-foot tub rested in the otherwise dark room. It was cold, though the windows were cloaked in fog from a steaming metal pot on the floor, the pot Grandma Estrella normally used for menudo. She told all of us to get on our knees and drape our heads, facedown, over the bathtub. The porcelain was chilly against my neck and arms. Grandma Estrella used to bathe me there when I was younger, working my knees and elbows with a washcloth and Ivory soap. Once, I asked her why she needed to scrub so hard it hurt. "Because we are not dirty people," she had said. Later, when I asked Mama about it, she told me when Grandma Estrella was a little girl, her own teachers called her a dirty Mexican and it never left her, the shame of dirt.

Slowly, from behind me, I felt Grandma Estrella pour bitter water over my head, a liquid made from something called neem that had a thick rootlike stench. Grandma then combed my short hair, harsh and fast, pressing into my scalp. When she finished, she told me to stand up.

"Mija, take this. Make sure to get the backside of their necks to the front side above their foreheads."

She placed the heavy pot in my hands. "But I don't think I can lift it."

. . . . . . .

"Don't be such a malcriada."

I braced myself, steadied my knees, and lifted the pot. My arms trembled as I poured the liquid over Harrison's small neck, seeing for the first time how incredibly scabbed and bitten he was.

"Does it hurt?" I asked.

"No, Clarisa," he said, muffled and soft. "I'm sorry they don't go away."

"Don't worry. This time it'll work."

As I finished pouring the water over Harrison's head, Grandma Estrella got on her knees and began rubbing his scalp with a white towel.

"Don't get it down my back," Mama said. She was tense against the tub, gripping the rim with white-knuckled hands. She kept looking back at me, squinting. That's when I noticed she was shaking, her legs and wrists trembling. Grandma Estrella had put down her white towel and was leaned over Mama. She reached out, letting her hands lightly rest on Mama's head, as if she was protecting her from the cold.

Grandma Estrella whispered, "That man and his choices are behind you now."

Mama said, "I just wanted him to know he has a sister."

"And now he does, my baby, but none of this is your place." She then danced her fingers over Mama's neck, motioning for me to begin pouring, wetting her skin along with Mama's.

The next day, Mama put on a full face of makeup, ran mousse through her lice-free hair, and dropped Harrison off at his apartment on Grant Street. I waited outside in the car, looking up at the window I knew was his. I wanted to catch a glimpse of him, my only brother in the world. I watched until he finally appeared. With his skinny arms, he reached up, and closed the blinds. It was the last time we dropped him off anywhere.

Before Grandma Estrella died, she gave me a booklet of all her remedies. Inside, with an unsteady hand she had drawn pictures of plants and, beneath them, their Spanish names, their scientific names, and just for me, their English names. I can cure head lice, stomach cramps, and bad breath with the right herbs. For the most part, I stick to over-the-counter remedies. They are cleaner and work faster and come in packages with childproof lids. But every once in a while, when I get a real bad headache and the aspirin isn't cutting it, I take slices of potatoes and hold them to my temples, hoping the bad will seep out of me.

I see Harrison every now and then in the city at parties or shows. He's a bass player in a punk band called the Roaches. He's tall now with a serious yet hopeful face. Sometimes I wonder if my dad looked like him as a young man when both our mothers fell for his shit. Other times, I wonder if he's still giving everyone lice. But I doubt it.

A couple months back, I was outside Lancer Lounge and through the windows I saw Harrison inside on the platform stage, bent over a microphone, a black cord rolled around his arm. When he stood up, we shared a look for a long time before I smiled, pointing to his blue Mohawk.

"Nice hair," I mouthed, and Harrison smiled back, as if he could hear me through the glass.

# Julian Plaza

. . . . . . . . . . . . . . . .

The lobby's hanging chalkboard announced all news—grandchild births, bingo nights, funeral services. As part of our recent after-school routine, Cora and I regularly checked the chalkboard, which was updated by our father, Ramón, the maintenance man of over a decade at Julian Plaza Senior Home. On a Monday afternoon in early spring, Cora tilted forward in her velvet romper and matching red scrunchie. She squinted as she read.

"Mrs. Flores! I knew it." Cora pretended to choke herself with both hands, her eyes flickering white globes. She claimed all old people died in order of who was poorest, sickest, and loneliest. "I liked that one. She didn't have crappy candy."

"Me, too," I said. "She always had Skittles."

The elevator doors chimed open behind us, and our father marched out, carrying an orange bucket filled with tools. His shoulders were broad in his gray flannel, the sleeves rolled, baring a faded eagle tattoo across his left forearm. With my light eyes and chestnut hair, I took after my father, whom my mother used to joke had the face of a conquistador—clover eyes, a long prominent nose, and a pointed Spanish chin from some long-lost Atencio ancestor. My father wore his auburn hair coiffed, and throughout the day it rocked nicely in a calm wave. He only used fine-tooth black combs and breezy Finesse shampoo. *Rinse and repeat, my babies,* he'd say. *That's how you get the smell to stick.*

"Oh, Papa," Cora said. "Mrs. Flores kicked it?"

"Don't say that. Polite thing to say is passed away, or—"

"Bites the dust? Keeled over?"

I giggled, but stopped when my father shot me a look.

"Don't encourage her, Alejandra. I need at least one civilized daughter." He edged back on his sand-colored work boots, directing his gaze toward the large clock in the front office. "Got a few more rounds." He disappeared into the main hallway, the green carpet and pink walls swallowing his frame.

Cora and I spent the afternoon in the basement rec room. No one was ever there and it always had a smell like rocks. There were several dated exercise machines, boxes of Chinese checkers, a cable TV, and aspen tree wallpaper. Cora challenged me to race on the stationary bikes, and despite the pointlessness, I said okay. She settled into a slinking cat–like stance, her long braided hair hanging over her left shoulder. Her sneakers were bright from thorough cleanings, but I could see the beginnings of a hole where an orange sock blinked.

After several minutes of screeching gears and exaggerated breathing, she said, "Do you think Papa loves one of us more than the other?"

She often asked questions like this, questions she'd answer herself. I kept pedaling.

Cora slid off her bike. She walked to the recliner by the television and took a seat. "It's pretty obvious he likes you better—for now—but I don't know about *loves* you better. That's much more complicated." She clicked on the TV, searching for Nickelodeon. "But you know what? He doesn't love either of us more than he loves Mama."

"You're supposed to love someone the most if they're sick," I said.

The previous December, my mother walked into the living room of our tiny 1920s home on Denver's Eastside. Cora and I were seated on the warped hardwood floor, drawing mermaids with colored pencils. Outside, on Twenty-sixth Street, it was sleeting. Through the dusty front windows, grayish light came into the living room and illuminated my mother in a lime-colored towel. She walked toward us, her wet black hair dripping down her shoulders and neck. It looked as if she was melting, a woman made of wax. She kneeled onto the floor and asked Cora to feel her left breast, but my sister refused with a sour face. My mother then turned to me. Without asking, she guided my hand beneath the towel, over her satiny skin, her invisible body hairs prickly against my fingers. "What does that feel like to you, Alejandra?"

"Where?" I asked.

"Here," she said, kneading my hand above her heart.

Her substantial breast was warm and firm, and nested inside was a jagged pit.

"Baby girl." My mother pinched her lips, hardening her features. "Please tell me what you feel."

"A rock, Mama. Beneath your skin."

Weeks later, my mother and father were at the kitchen table. Above them a moth flew inside a frosted light fixture, casting its caged shadow over their faces. Cora and I had wiggled across the hallway rugs, positioning ourselves belly-down above the staircase. We clung to the banister and peered through its splintered bars. My mother wore a blue nightdress, her plum-colored nipples visible through chiffon. The house felt musky and damp, and from somewhere in my gut I knew this was the air of fear.

My father kissed my mother's collarbones, held her slight wrists. "We'll be fine, Nayeli," he said. "We can find a way to afford better treatments." He stooped at my mother's side and appeared miraculously small laying his head in her lap. "Don't worry, mi querida."

My mother lifted her face into the light, her eyes focused somewhere near Cora and me. Cora ducked to the side, pulling me with her. As we stared at the rug, we heard our mother say, "They'll let you go if you start missing days."

"There are other jobs, ones with better insurance."

"No," my mother said. "It's too risky to quit. I'll go to Cynthia's when it's time."

Cora tugged on my left arm, edging us up from the floor. She had a severe, worried expression and her dark eyes were cloudy. "Why should Mama live there?" she whispered. "We can take care of her."


Miss Cynthia and her husband, a barber we called Uncle Rex, lived several blocks away in a house even older than ours. It had chipped teal paint and a long wooden wheelchair ramp that I liked to imagine was a pirate ship's plank. That evening, after we left Julian Plaza, Cora and I stood on their porch covered in thick vines and dried leaves while my father knocked on the red door.

"Oh, my little Atencio dollies," Miss Cynthia said as she

ushered us inside, a boy toddler on her hip. Miss Cynthia was a Castillo, an old Spanish name that my father said was somewhere on our family tree, though I didn't see a resemblance. Her black eyes were seeds behind round, scratched glasses and her hair was silver, braided in a bun at the nape of her neck. She was a thickset woman, her breasts weighing into her waistline. She always wore a rooster-print apron with lumpy pockets filled with pacifiers, and her sneakers were clunky and beige. Though she was old, Miss Cynthia was what my father called spry.

She led us through the kitchen, where cookies and baby food rested on the table. Across the checkered linoleum floor, we passed more toddlers playing with blocks and a plastic rocking horse. Miss Cynthia stepped over them and stopped at the back door, where my mother stayed.

"She's loopy today," she said to our father. "It's them new pills. They're no good." The boy toddler on Miss Cynthia's hip stared at me. When I waved, he turned away.

In the back room, before a three-paneled window, my mother sat in a used metal wheelchair, her head tilted lightly to the right, her wrists dangling over the armrests. She looked outside and appeared to watch the fruitless peach trees quiver in the yard. It was sunset, the sky gold and lavender. The room was built into the shape of a half-moon with its own outside entrance, as if Uncle Rex had built onto the house as an afterthought, an extra way to charge rent. My mother's sick things were displayed beside her on an aluminum tray. An airbrushed painting of the Virgin Mary, a pink phone with a curly cord, a pig-colored bedpan, school portraits of Cora and me, and many orange pill bottles.

"Hi, Mama," I said, soft and low.

My mother hummed and wetted her mouth with a sip of water. "Alejandra, the alley cat."

"Can I show you something?"

She bowed her head of loose hair.

Sitting at her feet, I pulled the chapter book from my backpack, showing her illustrations of Marcus, a greenish horse, riding a comet's tail. "He can fly into other animals' dreams."

"Ah." My mother spun her index finger in circles around my temple. "I can do that, too."

"Are you a bruja, Mama?"

She smiled with her eyes.

We sat around my mother like she was a tree, hooking onto her limbs, smoothing her scratchy Pendleton blankets. My father told stories of work—the new tenants, the old ones who had passed, and the renovations to the eighth-floor deck. After a while, he was quiet and let his forehead rest against her crown. Before my mother was sick, he often slid his arms around her waist as she cooked dinner. He sniffed her curls and kissed her shoulders and earlobes. She used to giggle, shaking him off, saying, "Stop that, Ramón, the babies don't want to see that."

My mother asked, "Where's Cora?"

She was in the corner, sitting on the bed, studying a tray of orange prescription bottles when my father motioned for her. Cora hopped down. She walked sluggishly to our mother, giving her one kiss on the cheek. She eventually told her how much she missed her, speaking first quietly and then more urgently, telling our mother she wanted her back home. "I wear your T-shirts to bed. I like the Betty Boop one."

My mother nodded several times, her eyelids lowering like a weighted baby doll's. She was suddenly in and out of sleep, snoring and whistling like the vents at Julian Plaza. Cora grimaced and retreated to the bed. She stayed there for the rest of our visit.

Before we left that evening, my father spoke to Uncle Rex.

He was in the main room, arched over a fat man in a black barber's cape. Uncle Rex was giving him a shave. He looked up and said hello to us with a flick of his razor. My father paused between an open set of French doors. "I'll check that bathroom light now, Rex."

Uncle Rex nodded, smoothing a puff of shaving cream over the fat man's neck.

My father then passed Miss Cynthia a handful of bills that she buried in her lumpy apron.


For dinner, my father made goulash. "Goddamn," he said, "it may be cheap, but, babies, it's good." He set the pot on the table and Cora and I slid over each of our bowls. My father spooned heaving plops of noodles and ground beef into the blue plastic. He then grunted and took his seat, unfolding a white paper napkin over his grimy jeans before we prayed.

"How was work today, Papa?" I asked.

"Not great," he said. "Mr. George Baker put in a call at noon for a dishwasher repair, but when I arrived, he didn't have a pulse. He was bent over the tub, naked as the day he came into this world. Except his socks. He had on those."

"How disgusting," Cora said, in between sips of water.

"It is what it is," my father said. "But that man had no one. Not a soul. It's a hard way to go—alone like that, but, my God, was he hoarding. Watches, coins, electronics, all kinds of stuff."

Cora looked up from her goulash. Though she appeared to have something she wanted to say, she only glanced out the window, then looked back at her noodles, sliding her fork's prongs through three of them.

I thought Mr. George Baker was one of the poorest men at Julian Plaza. He had moth-eaten suits, wilted fedoras, and no one ever visited him, something Cora explained was a whole 'nother type of poor. "Do you think he has a family?"

"Everyone has a family, Alejandra," my father said. "It just depends on whether that matters to them. I'd say it wasn't something Mr. Baker cared much about at all. Some men are like that. Real lone wolf types."

I imagined men in the mountains, wild with long hair and bloodied fangs for teeth. "I'm glad you're not like that, Papa."

My father chuckled—the creases around his eyes and mouth deepened. When we finished dinner, he kissed our hands and asked us to do the dishes. "If you need me," he said, "I'll be out back."

I washed while Cora stacked and dried. Through the window above the sink, I watched my father and a short man silhouetted against the garage light. They were looking at a television, walking around it, crouching down, pulling the cord straight. My father handed him a stereo and something else that was in a smallish cardboard box. The short man carried the items to his pickup and my father shut and locked the garage. I handed Cora a cup with an image of Tinker Bell, stuck, jamming her wide hips through a keyhole.

"You know, he steals all that stuff," she said. "From the dead old people."

"That's not true. Papa wouldn't do that."

Cora took the last dish from me. I turned off the faucet and watched my father take a handful of cash from the man.

"You don't know what anyone would or wouldn't do," Cora said. "You're just a baby. That's Mr. Baker's TV. I guarantee it."

Within a couple weeks, spring had shifted into the beginnings of summer. School had finally let out and Cora and I spent more time at Julian Plaza than ever. On a Monday in early June, my father's shift ended an hour early and he drove us to Miss Cynthia's in his small maroon pickup. He put on a Steely Dan CD as we rode along Park Avenue, the windows down, a warm breeze riding through our hair. The music was like a soundtrack to our neighborhood—little old ladies with white parasols, homeless men with spotted dogs, policemen on black bicycles in green vests, and all the other cars and trucks with headlights and grills like shining, optimistic faces. My father was singing "Dirty Work" when he pulled over outside of a big black Victorian house. He opened the truck's door and stepped onto the sidewalk, crossing a patch of grass until he stood beside a lilac bush. He retrieved his work knife from his back pocket, cutting off a branch. "Smell those babies," he said, as he stepped back inside the truck. "Your mama's favorite."

"Isn't that stealing?" Cora asked coolly from the front seat.

"Nah. They went over the sidewalk. It's a public service."

I laughed from the middle seat and my father winked before setting the flowers in my lap.


In bed, tiny beneath thick quilts, my mother smiled as we approached her side. My father presented his lilacs, arms out, as if he carried an exotic purple bird. "Pretty," she said, and my father placed the flowers on the mantel across the room, their lightness and sweet smell overpowering the stale stench of sickness. My mother uncoiled her palms, laying her hands open across the bed, as if she were absorbing our visit through her skin. We each took a turn with greetings and kisses. We rubbed her forehead, kissed her cheeks. She had recently lost so much weight that bones I never knew existed rose from her face, carving deep shadows around her eyes. Somehow, despite her body shrinking away, that afternoon it felt calm and restful in her room, as if the four of us were napping together in some enormous white bed.

After a long while, Miss Cynthia stepped through the back door, her rooster apron sashaying like gutter leaves caught in the wind. Cora and I moved to the window, where we sat on the long wooden bench. "She's due to be shifted," Miss Cynthia said and my father nodded. Cora and I watched as they considered my mother's body like a puzzle. With my father's help, Miss Cynthia maneuvered my mother onto her left side, propping pillows beneath her neck and arms, positioning her in a way that I imagined mermaids rested if they ever found themselves beached. "She isn't a high risk for bedsores," Miss Cynthia said to my father. "But you can never be too careful." I had no idea what bedsores were, but I pictured a bed with sharp teeth ready to puncture my mother's legs and hips, ripping full chunks from her body.

Once my mother was comfortable in her new position, Cora stood from the wooden bench and approached my mother with a small jar of Carmex from the side table. She dipped her pinkie inside and then ran her finger over our mother's lips. "You're chapped, Mama."

"My big helper Cora," she said, smacking her lips together and kissing the air.


That night I dreamed of my mother before she was sick. I was five years old and we were visiting my grandfather far away in a town called Saguarita, where my mother had grown up. The land was a wide valley surrounded by the bluest mountains with the whitest peaks. Cora and I were playing tag in the big field behind Grandpa Marcelo's tiny adobe home. The grown-ups watched from the lighted wooden porch. They were speaking softly and sipping beers, listening to Spanish songs on the radio, a strumming, sad guitar. Cora and I would turn back and wave to them before chasing each other again, twirling and giggling in all directions.

We had made it to the edge of the property, a place where a barbed-wire fence split the land in two. I was close to tagging Cora's arm, but she lunged to the side, her long black braid slithering through the air. That's when I stopped running and gasped at the sight of a baby deer very still in the tall grass, two bright lights for eyes. "Are you all alone?" I whispered. "Where is your mama?"

Cora stopped running, too, and she backtracked to stand beside me. "Maybe she was abandoned," she suggested. Cora smirked and I felt the edges of my mouth mirror hers. Like blackbirds silently shifting direction in midflight, in that moment we understood one another without words. We wanted to take that baby deer home with us, where it would sleep beneath our beds, graze throughout our yard, drink water from our tub. Our new sister, the animal. But we heard our mother then. She was sprinting in our direction, her hands gripping the bottom of her long yellow sundress as she shouted, "No, baby girls!" She looked taller and stronger than usual as she ran in strappy leather sandals. Even in twilight, I could see her face, determined and poised. She looked like fire burning her way across the valley.

By the time my mother had reached Cora and me, the baby deer had bolted to the other side of the barbed-wire fence. "Her mama is only out gathering food," my mother said, between heavy breaths. "I promise you. She'll come back."

———

The next morning, I found Cora on top of the garage. She was like a Christmas decoration in the middle of summer. Her hair was a black mess, unbrushed and unbraided. She paced in our mother's Betty Boop T-shirt, which fell past her knees. When I stepped into the backyard, she paused and lifted her arm, as though blocking a bright light. "What up, Alley Cat?"

"Can I come up?"

Cora pretended to yawn. "Walk over by the fence. I'll help you."

I could see our entire neighborhood. The mountains, my elementary school, Julian Plaza with its middle floors surrounded by a ring of green treetops. The clouds sagged over the city like a blanket of air. Cora stood beside me, her hand resting on her hip, her eyes scanning the city. She pointed toward Colfax Avenue with its hurried traffic, lined by motels and bars.

"Mama's over there," she said. "Behind the Burger King."

"It doesn't even look that far," I said.

"I know," Cora said. "She should be home with us."

"Mama can't live with us," I said. "Who would take care of her?"

"I can. I'm probably much better at it than Miss Cynthia. What does she know, anyway?"

I thought about how before my mother left, from the living room window, Cora and I watched her collapse in the front yard as she went to get the mail. We both waited a moment, as if she'd stand up and brush herself off. When she didn't, we ran outside without our shoes and coats. We tried to lift her and bring her inside, and when that didn't work, we attempted to drag her thin body into the house. We lived on a block where lawnmowers and bikes were stolen from garages in broad daylight, but no one walked by to help us. I cried and lay next to her while Cora ran inside and called our father from the kitchen. He drove home from Julian Plaza in record time.

"I think Miss Cynthia's a good lady," I said. "She does Mama's hair and gives her nice blankets."

"Look, she only takes care of Mama because she's getting paid. She doesn't care about her. She cares about money." Cora then slinked with one slender leg and then the other onto the wooden fence. "Come on, Alley Cat. We need to get ready."

"You's walked all the way here?" Miss Cynthia asked, scooting a plate of sugar cookies over her kitchen table in our direction. Her glasses were coated in dust. Two wiry black hairs poked out above her top lip and she had a toddler I hadn't seen before in her lap, a little girl gnawing her entire hand, her forearm covered in drool. Miss Cynthia wiped the baby's mouth with her rooster apron.

"Yeah," Cora said, refusing a cookie. "It isn't far."

"And you didn't get lost? I mean, you and the baby girl just found your way on your own?"

"We've been coming here for months. We know the way."

Miss Cynthia broke a cookie against the table and offered some to the baby. "Smart girl. I'm not sure if you're more like your mama or papa."

"She's like both," I said, biting into my cookie. "We both are like both."

Miss Cynthia smiled. Some teeth were brown with black gaps. She held her grin for too long and rose from the table, setting the toddler on the linoleum floor. The tot stood wobbly for a moment before crawling to the plastic rocking horse in the hallway. Miss Cynthia stood next to the telephone and adjusted a crucifix with baby Jesus nailed to the cross. He bled pink around his crown of thorns. "Listen, girls, your mama isn't well today. She's been having an especially rough morning. Her sickness is in her bones, now. It's everywhere."

Cora said she understood.

"Don't you want to wait for your papa? He brings you over almost every day, anyway. That way you can be with them both."

"No," Cora said. "We'd like to see our mother right now. Thank you."

Miss Cynthia lifted the plate of sugar cookies from the table, setting them down again on a countertop. "If you insist. Your mother is in the back room, in bed."

Cora and I had been around sick and dying people our entire lives. People, we learned, weren't permanent, and neither were their illnesses. When I was six years old and Cora was eight, our mother regularly visited a woman named Billy at Julian Plaza who had long, droopy ears and one leg. Cora told me the leg was chopped off because of a disease that made your limbs die before the rest of you did. Once, while we watched *The Price Is Right* with Billy, Cora looked away from the spinning wheel and said, "If doctors wanted to take my leg, I'd try to get it run over by a train or a bus." My mother shrieked and apologized for Cora. Billy died later that year, but I never forgot how her apartment smelled, like dirt inches below a garden's surface, where roots twirl into one another. That day at Miss Cynthia's, I sniffed the air and realized my mother's room smelled exactly like that.

The blinds were closed and the room was dim. My mother lay in her rented hospital bed beneath many colorful quilts. Wisps of hair curled around her forehead like tiny, black worms.

. . . . . . .

Her entire face seemed deflated, drained of blood. Cora twisted open the blinds. A plane of white light spread into the room and my mother's eyelids fluttered. I sat beside her, stroking her forehead. She felt cool and damp, the way I imagined a snail feels inside its shell. "Hi, Mama," I whispered close enough for my lips to touch her ear.

She blinked and looked at me with eyes so black they resembled the spaces between stars. "I was supposed to get you from school."

"It's summertime," Cora said, pushing the wheelchair to our mother's bed. She bent down, unfolding the footrests and adjusting the handles. "We told you last time, Mama. School's been out for a while."

My mother reached for Cora's face. Her nails had been painted a bright, strawberry red by Miss Cynthia. They were short, studded berries that moved along Cora's head, petting her like an animal. My mother winced. "It's hard to keep track of the weather," she said and rolled onto her side. She closed her eyes, letting out a long, guttural moan.

Cora said, "You shouldn't be here. You've only gotten sicker. I knew it would make you worse. No one listens to me."

My mother bit the edge of her pillow, her teeth sinking into the case. She spoke in murmurs and groans.

"We can't understand you," Cora said.

"Babies." She breathed. "Can you get—" She cried out. "Miss Cynthia?"

Cora looked as though she'd been struck. She shook her head and reached for the bed's remote. I asked her not to, and tugged on her arm. She pushed me off and raised the mattress until our mother sat upright, the quilts falling to her waist. It looked as though her limbs had evaporated. I pressed her sleeve, expecting only air. She looked confused and small like a feverish child home sick from school. I scooted off the bed and I stared at the hump of her feet—shivering and slight—beneath the quilts. I placed my hand over her right foot.

"She's not feeling good," I told Cora.

"That's why she's leaving," Cora said. "That's why we're taking her."

Cora hunched over and slipped her hands beneath our mother's side. With a jerk of her neck, she gestured for me to do the same.

"I don't know," I said. "She hurts."

"It'll be easy. Remember when Papa did it? He lifted her like a baby."

"Fine," I said, doing what Cora asked, positioning myself against my mother's hip.

Cora nodded. "All right, Alley Cat. One. Two. Three. Lift."

My mother's body rose from the mattress. Her pelvis poked my palms and her nightgown pulled straight behind her. We had her. She was in our hands, rising to the roof like smoke. We could carry her. It was possible. She'd glide home in her wheelchair, beautiful and thin, elegant in the sunlight. But my mother opened her eyes and I saw how far we'd really gone. Nowhere at all. With a frightened jolt, she wailed and squirmed. Cora lost her grip first, placing my mother's deadweight on me until we both flopped against the bed, the metal handrail, the plastic remote. I let go and backed away as my mother cried out, over and over.

The door opened then and Miss Cynthia stepped into the room. She walked behind the wheelchair with her rooster apron hanging loosely over her legs. She stared at us, her glasses white with light and her mouth a gaping black hole. "What in God's name."

———

When Miss Cynthia told our father what we had done, he drove us home in silence, his disappointment thick as he leaned into turns and idled at red lights. The street was like a horse's long back, dark with specks of light. I went to bed that night listening to the sounds of Cora crying quietly on the other side of the wall. I tried reading more about the horse named Marcus, but everything he did seemed suited for a cartoon, something enjoyable, something fake. Cora tapped her wall a couple times, code for me to enter her room, and I stepped through the darkness and lay down in her twin bed. Her long hair was wetly matted against her Little Mermaid pillowcase. She pulled me close to her and said, "Don't worry. We'll figure out another way to get her. I promise."

But Cora didn't have to find a new way to bring our mother home, because not long after, while the three of us were at Julian Plaza—my father on his knees, pulling white hairs from drains, and Cora and me watching Nickelodeon in the rec room—our garage was robbed, the thieves taking everything my father sold to pay Miss Cynthia.

That evening, my father pulled into the back driveway and sat for a long while staring at the open garage door. He finally stepped out and inspected the busted lock. He crouched down, yanked blades of grass from the ground, and let them blow away in the wind, as if they'd point him in the direction of the thief.

At dinner, my father sat very still at the kitchen table. He breathed into a clenched fist. He kissed the tops of our heads and smoothed our hair. His work shirt was torn at the elbow, and his stubble inked over his chin and cheeks. "We're bringing Mama home in the next few days. It's going to be tough. I'll have to work most days, but I know my girls can take care of her while I'm away."

"I'll stay with her every day," Cora said.

My father covered his face with both hands. He stood from the table and walked to the bathroom. We heard the sink running, and beneath the sounds of rushing water, a long, guttural sob.

A few days later, a heat wave moved into the city. Sweaty children rushed the streets in ripped-up shorts and cotton tanks. Cora and I watched them from Julian Plaza's lobby, where we sat in black plastic chairs. Above them, the day moon was a sliver of a fingernail. Cora fanned herself with a Christian newsletter, dropped off earlier by a black woman in a blue skirt clear to the floor. The hanging chalkboard only announced an ice cream social and the birth of a grandchild named John Michael.

"I'm bored," Cora said.

"Do you want to play outside?" I asked.

Cora allowed her legs to dangle back and forth to the beat of the ticking clock. "Hydrant water is dirty." She slid further down in her chair, surprising me when she asked, "What else do you want to do, Alley Cat?"

I thought about the rec room, the Chinese checkers, the TV. We could eat packets of coffee creamer, pour sugar in rows for ants, toss rocks into the dumpsters. None of it seemed worthwhile. "Want to race?"

Cora dropped the Christian newsletter to the floor. She sat up and smiled. "We'll run each floor until we get to the top." She paused before saying, "On your mark, get set—"

"Go," I yelled.

We started down the hallway, and I pretended the green carpets were grass while the ceiling lights were rays of sunlight. After zigzagging up to the next floor and the floor after that, we came to a level with nearly all apartment doors open. It was swampy hot. Tenants sat in their crammed one-bedroom apartments, their metal fans blowing with wisps of paper. I saw an orange couch. I saw macramé wall art. I saw a lone silver head leaning into a bowl of soup. Some watched black-and-white movies, the volume at full blast. Maidens in white tied to railroad tracks. Cowboy heroes shot dead.

As we raced through every floor, zigzagging through Julian Plaza's ancient insides, I remembered a time when I was very little and my mother wasn't sick. It was summer and she wore a brown print dress and tall loud sandals with gardenia perfume and olive oil in her hair. She carried me on her slender hip while Cora walked beside us. We were visiting old people to give them pies—apple and rhubarb, strawberry and pecan. The pies weren't for everyone, just those without family, the people who needed them most. My mother knocked, and when each door opened, the people of Julian Plaza beamed with happiness, as if they'd never seen a young woman so lovely in all their long lives.

# GALAPAGO

. . . . . . . . . . . . . . . . .

The day before Pearla Ortiz killed a man, she had lunch at home with her granddaughter Alana. They sat together at the aluminum table in the small canary-yellow kitchen and ate turkey wraps with a wet kale salad. Alana had stopped by on her lunch break. She worked downtown in a glass high-rise for a marketing firm specializing in oil and gas and was dressed plainly in a brown shift dress, her lightened hair pulled high in a ponytail. Pearla watched Judy Garland sing in black and white on the television above the refrigerator and methodically chewed kale her dentures couldn't easily break down. She preferred her usual, flour tortillas with beans and rice, but she had learned to humor her granddaughter, who despite her prickliness, was good-hearted in her own way.

"We'll look at a few communities this week, get an idea of what's out there." Alana pushed a brochure across the table. She explained that it was for a senior home called Wellspring Acres, the print too small and too pale for older eyes.

. . . . . . .

Alana had been suggesting for years that Pearla sell her home on Galapago and rent an apartment in a building for seniors. The Denver housing market was booming, Alana often said, and retirement homes were much more chic than they used to be. Even houses on the Westside were going for a half million dollars. But Pearla had been on Galapago for sixty-two years, since she married Avel, when they were the first in the family, on either side, to own property.

"Gramma, did you hear me?" Alana took a swig of water and used her thumb to clean a smudge on the glass. She spoke louder. "It's more social, easier to take care of."

Pearla spit a ragged piece of kale into her palm. She nodded before turning back to Judy Garland. "That poor girl. How the world just ate her up."

Alana stood from the table. She clicked off the television. "Let's focus, Gramma."

Pearla laughed. Her granddaughter looked so bossy in her career clothes, but whenever Pearla looked at her, *really* looked at her, she still saw Alana as an eight-year-old girl who had come to live with her grandparents on Galapago Street after her mother, Mercedes, died. Alana arrived with nothing more than a suitcase filled with stuffed animals and chapter books. Managing household grief became another task as endless as chores. Avel sometimes cried beneath the forked apple tree in the backyard, and to hide his sorrow from Alana, Pearla would close the windows and turn up the country music station, drowning out everything with a twang. Now, thirty years later, Pearla wondered if she should have let Alana hear him cry.

After they finished lunch, Alana dutifully walked Pearla to her bedroom, a dark space between the kitchen and living room where the windows had long ago been boarded up. In that little room, lighted by lamps, Alana got to work making the queen-size bed. Pearla was embarrassed. There wasn't a day in her life she let a bed go unmade, but when her hands were particularly arthritic, she had trouble straightening the sheets and turning the quilt. She stood near the doorway, over the crushed pink carpet, and smiled as Alana finished, prideful as she fluffed pillows.

"You'd think I'd get a smaller bed, since Avel's been gone all these years," Pearla said.

Alana reached out, lightly smoothing her grandmother's white curls. "Long as you're comfortable, Gramma."

Before she headed back to work, they stood on the cement porch for a moment, the day unexpectedly pleasant for early March. Pearla gazed beyond Alana's shoulders at the rows of Westside houses, evenly spaced with wide porches and tiny square lawns. They were stout homes, some colorful, some beige, with chain-link fences and barred windows. There were old street signs reserving parking spots for the elderly, handicapped neighbors. But most of those folks were gone. While Pearla was once friendly with everyone on Galapago Street, now she knew almost no one. In the past decade, couples with expensive cars and Anglo names had moved onto the block, altering the houses and gutting the yards, once hacking down old Mrs. Archuletta's prized peach tree in a single afternoon.

"I have no interest in leaving, mija," Pearla said, before kissing Alana goodbye. "Hell, the Lord will take me soon enough."


The District 7 Police Station was busy at six in the morning. Clerks drank coffee and shuffled papers while criminals and victims shuffled in and out of fluorescent-lit hallways. Pearla sat for some time in a waiting room beside a stack of *Good Housekeeping* magazines and a fake plant that looked like a mini aspen tree. Alana arrived just before the detective called them back. She had applied a full face of makeup. She was shaking, much more than Pearla, and had a dazed look about her as she clutched her black leather jacket close to her chest.

"The only crime committed was armed burglary," said the detective, a middle-aged man with clever eyes inside a very big head. His name was Ralph Vigil and he had a jovial belly, like a melon beneath his dress shirt. His office was a white cubicle with flattened brown carpet, the only decoration a free Mexican restaurant calendar, a month behind, pinned to the felt wall. He began speaking to Pearla and Alana from behind a cherrywood desk but soon stood and rolled his chair beside Pearla. He swayed forward as he spoke, his arms resting on his bony knees. "The locks were busted on the back door. The nine-millimeter tucked into the young man's waistband was loaded. Case closed."

A gun? How had Pearla mistaken a gun for a knife? She stared at her reflection in the silver badge clipped to the detective's front pocket. Her face was long with clear hollows, and her once-dark hair was now a white nest. Without her usual rouge or lipstick, she appeared a ghastly gray, as if she were living in a black-and-white movie. Pearla cleared her throat to make her voice seem strong. She asked, "How old was he?"

"Nineteen," the detective said. "We get kids in here as young as fourteen who have shot up entire families, sometimes for nothing more than an Xbox. Count yourself lucky, ma'am."

"Oh Christ." Alana threw her arms around Pearla.

"The city is in flux, ladies. Lots of mixed income levels. They say things will cool down once the area is fully gentrified, but I'm skeptical."

"It's always been bad. I don't see how it can change," said Alana.

"You a Westside girl, Ms. Ortiz?"

"Born and raised, but now I'm in Highlands."

"You mean the Northside? ¿Como que Highlands?"

They laughed at that popular T-shirt slogan Pearla had seen young people wearing. Since the newcomers had started moving to Denver, they'd changed the neighborhood names to fit their needs, to sound less dangerous, maybe less territorial.

Pearla said, "You still haven't told me his name, Mr. Vigil."

"Cody." The detective flicked a nondairy creamer packet into his coffee. The white powder clumped together and sank to the bottom. "Cody Moore."

Crime was always part of the Westside. Their first break-in was in 1956, summertime. Newlyweds, Pearla and Avel walked home from Benny's dance hall, their arms linked. It was a cool night, the moon a slit of light. Avel's unruly hair was greased to shine, leaving smears across Pearla's neck as he kissed her on their cement porch. Sliding his callused palms beneath her salmon dress, he unlatched her stockings and guided apart her thighs. They entered the house, ready to make love right there on the living room floor but found the room ransacked. The thief had taken a box of silver jewelry from inside the bedroom closet. The next day, Avel and his cousin Benito welded iron bars over the windows. Pearla began doing housework in the mornings to avoid the afternoon shadows that fell upon her home like a cage. For over twenty years she sought out the stolen silver in pawnshops, once reclaiming a turquoise cuff from the glass case at an antique shop on South Broadway. "Lovely piece," the Anglo saleswoman said. "It'll look wonderful with your coloring."

The second break-in was autumn of 1978. Pearla and Avel

were recovering from the hurt that their only child, Mercedes, had gone a bad way. She was addicted to alcohol and barbiturates, hitchhiking from town to town across the Southwest. In Bisbee, Arizona, after going to an all-night club with a dirt floor, she slept with a man whom she only remembered as having one blue eye and one green. Pregnant with Alana, she returned to Denver, got a little apartment, a respectable job selling office supplies on Sixteenth Street, and threw herself a baby shower that was only attended by her parents and her best friend, a warmhearted gay man named Miguel Orlando. Within a decade, both Miguel and Mercedes would be dead—she of hepatitis and Miguel of AIDS—but the shower was beautiful. The four of them devoured far too many tamales and slices of tres leches cake, the party going until after midnight as they shared family stories and their aspirations for the baby inside Mercedes.

"It's going to be a girl," Avel said to Pearla, back home on their porch swing. "A strong one." He slid off his cowboy boots, allowing them to air out in the night. For a moment, the couple sat with their joy. When Pearla headed inside, nothing was unusual about the house until she entered the bedroom. In the far corner, broken glass glinted across the oak floor. Squinting upward, Pearla looked to the shattered window, where a small child was perched between the iron bars, its legs dangling as if it sat in a tree. The child stared at Pearla, the light inside its eyes suspended as it swooped from the window ledge, fading into the alley, taking with it the diamond necklace Avel had given Pearla after hitting the jackpot on what he thought, at the time, was a lucky slot machine in Central City.

The next morning, Pearla asked Avel to nail wooden boards over the bedroom window, blocking from the room both thieves and sunlight. It took some getting used to, but the darkness grew on Pearla. She draped the boards with pink satin and decorated the walls with colorful, gauzy scarves. One night, after the boards were up for nearly two years, Pearla dreamed of the child with light eyes, its legs sliding beneath the satin, moving like tentacles over everything in sight. Pearla then purchased a silver-plated pistol and placed it in her stockings drawer, never believing she would actually fire it.

A week after the shooting, though Alana had paid for a professional cleaning service, Pearla still found blood dried between cracks in the kitchen walls. She made a solution from vinegar and salt, sponging away the brown mess as she waited for her granddaughter. They were to visit a senior home, a community called St. Lorena, no saint Pearla had ever heard of, but it had been decided after the young man's death that Pearla was leaving Galapago, and that was that.

As she hunched over and cleaned the walls, Pearla fought her mind's tendency to drift. In the canary-yellow kitchen, the lace curtains rising and falling from brass vents gushing heat, she saw Cody Moore's stomach muscles in a defined V as he reached for what she thought was a knife. His fingernails were wide and chewed, and his saucerlike green eyes were dryly blank. How had she not noticed it was a gun? Was Pearla that blinded by old age? And did it change things that, like her, the boy was carrying a weapon? Knives killed people all the time, but guns killed them more. One thing Pearla was certain of. She was ashamed that even in her old age, she wanted to live more than die.

After she had finished in the kitchen, Pearla dropped the sponge into a trash can and went outside to gather the day's mail. She accidentally marked a bundle of coupons in reddish brown fingerprints as she waited on the porch for her granddaughter to arrive.

"The most noticeable thing about our residents is their collective smile."

Alana and Pearla listened to a tour guide, a young redhead in a goofy kitty sweater. They were paused in the lobby of St. Lorena, overlooking the ice of Sloan's Lake. Everything was vanilla-hued with mahogany trim. Skylights illuminated the hallways, where residents curved over aluminum walkers. The tour guide pointed out the wooden rocking chairs facing the mountains, the baby grand piano in the recently renovated dining hall, and the locally designed iron screens over the brick fireplaces.

Pearla asked if there was a Catholic church nearby.

"Certainly, and Mass is performed in Spanish two times per day. Noon and five o'clock."

"We speak English," Alana said, matter-of-factly.

The tour guide looked as though she wanted to apologize.

Pearla said, "Thank you, pumpkin. Church is important to me."

The next stop on the tour was an apartment belonging to a seventy-eight-year-old woman who was visiting her grandchildren in Lake Tahoe. It was a studio with stucco walls and taupe carpets. A twin bed, covered with a childish purple comforter, occupied space in the far corner, beneath a painting of a blond Jesus. The tour guide explained that the apartment was a popular choice for *independent elderly women* rather than using the word *widow*.

"Where does she keep all her things?" Pearla asked. "Her furniture, her clothes?"

The tour guide relaxed her face. She had kind green eyes.

"Learning to separate ourselves from unnecessary clutter is one of the hardest aspects of transitioning out of an independent living situation and into a community home."

Pearla said she had no more questions, and they moved on to the cafeteria, where a rack of gray roast beef warmed beneath a heat lamp.

Alana was late.

"You drag yourself to Mass this morning?"

She told her grandmother not to start with any church talk.

They drove the freeway to the cemetery without conversation, the radio on a news program. As they entered Mt. Olivet's iron gates, clouds seemed to clear and sunshine brightened the headstones and mausoleums. They first drove by the graves belonging to rich folks, those with marble angels and stone beacons. All her life, Pearla had put aside money for a respectable grave, prematurely using the money for Mercedes, giving her daughter a proper stone. Her own parents were buried in the desert with only wooden crosses to mark their bones. The crosses decayed over time, crouching into the earth, until one summer, on a road trip to the San Luis Valley with Avel and Mercedes, Pearla couldn't locate her mama's and papa's graves anymore. She left wildflowers and sage near a mile marker that seemed close enough.

"They don't mow regularly?" Alana asked, prying crabgrass from her grandfather's grave. Pearla's own headstone was beside it, an open dash for her death date.

"Not on our side," Pearla said, referring to what the archdiocese used to call the Spanish section. It was near what were once referred to as the Oriental and Negro sections, across the tracks from the suicides and unbaptized babies. The rules weren't enforced anymore, but families were buried near one another and so things stayed intact.

Pearla rummaged through a plastic grocery sack on her side. She pulled out washrags and spray bottles. She handed some to Alana. "Start with his name and the dates. I'll get the back side."

The vinegar solution spread into the headstone, releasing an odor like rust. Alana was decent and kind, arching her back and rolling up her coat sleeves before she scrubbed. Pearla had to give the girl that. She had never been lazy. Always a hard worker.

Avel's headstone was soon brighter than it had been. The wind was calm as Pearla placed plastic marigolds beneath his name, the orange petals only slightly wavering against the yellow grass. The women then prayed the rosary, the hard beads slick in their hands.

From a distance, the section of the cemetery where Mercedes was buried seemed like an empty field. It was only standing directly above the graves that Pearla could read any names. Destiny Dixon, Sabrina Cordova, Susana Mullins, and there, toward a chain-link fence beside the train tracks, Mercedes Angelica Ortiz. Pearla loathed standing over graves, worried she was stepping on a face or a chest. Maybe it was because when she was a little girl, a priest had once told her that hell was really just a grave.

"Hi, Mama," Alana whispered. She kneeled and yanked massive weeds from the flat headstone's corners, the roots held by frozen dirt. Years ago, she had spoken of buying a nicer plot for her mother, but over time she had changed her mind or, worse, maybe she had forgotten. "We miss you, Mama. We miss you so much."

Pearla cupped her mouth with both hands, holding in a choking cry as she stood on the dead grass above her daughter's feet. She always expected Avel to go first, it seemed the usual way, but when Mercedes passed, it stole something from inside her, a bone she couldn't quite name. "I pray for you, my baby. Every day."

On the drive home, Alana said, "We have a move-out date for you, April first."

"If your grandfather was alive, mija, he would be ashamed to live anywhere but our home." Pearla glanced out the window at identical housing developments rolling over the foothills. They reminded her of locusts, devouring the land. "I hope he doesn't somehow see any of this."

Alana seemed stunned, taking her eyes off the road, almost looking directly at her grandmother. "Some drug addict came into your house with a gun and tried to kill you. You're not staying there, Gramma, and that's the end of it."

Pearla went quiet then. She wondered about Cody. Was his body in a cemetery? Was it near a freeway or train tracks? Did he have, at the very least, some flowers? Even plastic would do.

The night it happened Pearla dreamed of a memory, only different. She was seven years old and still lived in Saguarita, where her papa worked the mines. They had a company house, a one-room cabin without electricity or heat. The floor was dirt and the ceiling was patched with grass where, sometimes, blue sky winked and snow drifted down onto their bed quilts. Pearla ran between the mountains, the land beneath her feet jagged with quartz and sagebrush, her little body a blur of white lace and black braids. It was church Sunday and she was late. When Pearla's legs couldn't carry her any faster, the wind picked up and she lifted over pine trees and the mirrored ponds, where she saw herself sailing toward that adobe steeple with her arms open to the land.

Pearla awoke at half past two when the pressure in her gut surged all the way to her throat. For a moment, she sat motion-less in bed, surrounded by rosaries and unlit candles across her nightstand. Pearla reached for her flannel robe, laid out beside her on the mattress, but a feeling stopped her. She held her breath and listened. There was something in the kitchen, a small metallic rattling, the creak of redistributed weight. The sounds entered Pearla's body like a vibration in her bones rather than her ears. Pearla prayed. She asked for help from everyone, Mer-cedes, Avel, her mama and papa. A vision came to her, a young Anglo man with an exhausted heart, nearly dead as he shivered in a room without windows, without lights.

*Don't aim a gun,* Avel had once told her, *unless you're pre-pared to kill what's standing in front of it.*

With her robe buttoned clear to her throat, Pearla reached for the silver-plated pistol in her stockings drawer, her heart beating so loudly that she feared it would be overheard through her rib cage. Pearla walked into the kitchen, where a young man was bent over, fumbling with the locks on the basement door, the stove's electric light shining across his shaved head. When he turned to face Pearla, for a long second their eyes met. How dull and vacant. How wasted and long. There was nothing of great value in the house, the basement in particular. Only old paint cans and fishing nets with rusted metal handles. What an unfor-tunate misunderstanding. Time began to move oddly, slowly and flat. Pearla was certain Avel would be coming through the front door at any moment. The young man would run off, down the alley. The old couple would talk of saving money, taking in laundry or boarders, anything to afford a home in a better neighborhood. Maybe north toward the Italians on Lowell or east toward the Jews by the university. Anywhere but Galapago.

But that life was done.

The young man snapped into movement, reaching for something in his waistband, a knife with a dark blade. Pearla shivered in pink slipper-socks, her pistol aimed. She said, *Please, please*. The young man could not focus—it looked as though his eyes were borrowing his body. He stepped forward once. There was a blue sparrow tattooed on his right forearm, a name written beneath the wings. When Pearla pulled the trigger, the young man's body went lax and dropped to the linoleum floor as reddish spray exited his right side, splattering the eggshell kitchen walls.

"I aimed low for his legs," Pearla told the 911 dispatcher. Gasping between tears, she repeated, "I aimed low."

Alana cleared Pearla's vanity, pulling photos of Mercedes and Avel from the mirror and placing them in a shoe box. She had already packed most of the kitchen while Pearla stood by, watching in wonder, as her granddaughter tossed out expired boxes of pancake mix and old jars of Mrs. Archuletta's peaches. She was moving in three days.

Pearla shuffled around in the bedroom's lamplight, taking stock of what she needed. She had drawers filled with dried Revlon nail polish, tubes of coral lipstick worn down to stubs, empty bottles of Chanel No. 5, but what was empty when you could always squeeze out another drop? The closet was jammed with hand-sewn dresses, worn decades ago at some dance or baptism. Beneath the bed were boxes of hats that had long ago

gone out of style, come back in, and gone out again. Avel's cowboy boots lined the closet floor, a pointed row of ancient leather.
All of it junk, and all of it precious.

Alana said, "I know it's hard, Gramma, only taking what
you need."

"It's not like I'll take any of it with me when I'm dead," said
Pearla with some hesitation. "Might as well start now."

Alana asked her grandmother why she must say such morbid
things.

Pearla flapped her hands in the air, as if to say, *What, how do
you mean?* She then lifted an amethyst necklace from her vanity. It was a gift from Avel the year before he died, a small heart-
shaped stone with golden roses along the sides. Pearla looked
deeply into the stone's color and noticed it had changed into
something warmer, brighter, but she soon realized that it was
only a ray of sunlight. Following the warm line, she discovered
a small, roundish hole had developed in the wooden boards
covering her bedroom windows. Pearla pushed aside the pink
satin and examined the wood, smoothing her palms over the
brittle surface.

"Mija," she said with sudden urgency, "let's get this down."

Deep inside the closet, Alana retrieved a hammer from Avel's
orange toolbox. She jimmied out the rusted nails bottom to top
until the dusty boards dropped with a crash and, for the first
time in forty years, the bedroom was flooded with light.

# CHEESMAN PARK

. . . . . . . . . . . . . . . . .

I told the bank manager I was leaving Los Angeles for Denver because I missed my mother and the mountains and that while California was beautiful, it was too crowded and expensive. She hugged me with her bony body, smelling of watery coffee and mint. "Back to the Mile High you go," she said. "You were always a team player, Liz." That evening, as I carried a box of my things to the car, rust-colored fog cloaked the parking lot. The reflection of my face was blurred in my driver's side window. My hands trembled as I got in my car and thought of the real reason I was leaving and wept.


I grew up in North Denver with my mother and father. They met in their mid-twenties, kids who lived to drink and play pool, occasionally snorting cocaine when they could afford it. I admired them—my outgoing mother with black 1960s Hollywood hair and my father with his gentle green eyes and a confident work-boot gait. But as much as I loved them, they also terrified me, my father in particular. He once hurled a sack of groceries filled with jars of strawberry jam and maraschino cherries at my mother's jaw. Other times, he just used his fists. *It's not his fault*, my mother would tell me, painting a picture of his childhood in Detroit, where one night his schizophrenic father shot his mother and then turned the gun on himself.

The winter I turned thirteen, my father left us for another woman. I cried myself to sleep for six months. My mother did the same until we moved into a two-bedroom apartment overlooking Cheesman Park. "Always remember," she said the day we unpacked. "This is our home." But I didn't feel at home and, when I was nineteen, I moved to California with hopes of modeling or doing commercials—people often said I possessed striking "exotic" features. It didn't work out. I got a job as a bank teller. I went out every night and I learned to recognize faces under barroom red lights. I often found myself in the company of drug addicts and midwest runaways. I usually had two or more unsteady boyfriends at a time. I always felt alone. One night, as I leaned over the wooden rail along the Santa Monica Pier, breathing in that ripe fragrance of sea and salt, I gazed into the rolling black tide, wondering what it would take for me to finally return home.

"Come here, mija," my mother said. "Let me get a look at your face."

I stood in her front room, my skin covered in an oily sheen and my mouth sour from the sixteen-hour drive. My mother eased herself out of the wooden rocking chair. She took my face in her waxy hands, turning my chin from side to side. She grimaced, deepening the line between her penciled-in eyebrows.

"You should have seen me a week ago," I said. "My face looked like rotting fruit."

My mother shook her head, her black hair in a bun, a silver line streaking behind her left ear. "You're as beautiful as ever, Liz."

My bedroom was the same as when I was a teenager—coral walls, mirrored closet doors, and a twin bed beneath a window that overlooked the park with its stone pavilion and rolling greenery. The park lights had come on. The damp asphalt shed steam as though the entire park was vaporously lifting into the sky.

"I never got around to changing it," said my mother. "I had all these plans. I wanted to get a treadmill in here, maybe turn it into an office, but who knows, I said, maybe my daughter will come home someday. Then she won't want to sleep on a printer."

We laughed and my mother began fluffing pillows, straightening sheets. She was still beautiful with wet eyes and a long unlined neck, though her movements had slowed in recent years. She was a woman who adhered to order. Life had a schedule. Things needed to be cleaned. Rules needed to be followed.

"There's room for all your things in the closet and the storage space is open in the basement." She flicked on a brass lamp at my bedside, and I saw her eyes settle on my face. "Have you thought about what I said, about getting a job?"

"Thought I'd take a few weeks off. Get my mind straight."

My mother stepped away from the bed. She stood on her tiptoes and kissed my forehead. "Make sure you find something to do, something to be proud of. You've got to stop thinking about it."

———

The man I had been sleeping with in Los Angeles was alone for the weekend, his fiancée in San Francisco visiting family. We were in bed when I told him it wasn't fair, that I loved him, that I often cried. *Leave her,* I said while he choked me as he always did during sex. He said nothing and I bucked, drawing blood from his face with my nails. A lamp broke. The room went dark. It wasn't out of the ordinary, but then it was. He slapped my face into the wall, chipping a tooth and breaking my nose. I heard the brittle crack replay again and again as I staggered outside.

I drove to my apartment with my dress inside out, my hand cupped over my bloody mouth. Two officers responded to my 911 call. One was a woman in lip gloss, a French manicure on her fingernails. In my pink bathroom, I wore a lacy bra and black panties as she snapped photos of my injuries. Afterward, she gave me a pamphlet on victims' rights. I had never called 911 before and as I stood there half naked and shivering, I wished that I hadn't. A detective called the next morning. In a booming, breezy voice, he told me he understood how scared I must be, but pressing charges would mean a trial. It could take weeks, months, to convict this guy. It'll be tricky, he explained, especially since you two weren't technically dating. I eventually agreed. What I wanted most, I told him, was to go home.

"Good choice," he said. "By the way. I'm looking at your pictures right now. You're Spanish or something, right? You could be a model. Something in those eyes."

Most days that summer I woke up to the sounds of my mother. She was an academic counselor at a community college and left early, sometimes at dawn. I'd hear her in the bathroom flushing the toilet, clearing her throat into the sink, and singing Spanish songs in the shower. After I was alone, I'd walk the building, reacquainting myself with the boiler room, the basement's stone slits for windows, and the locked storage units that resembled oversize ovens. The only magnificent area was the roof. A broken emergency exit opened to a view in every direction. To the west was the jagged crust of the mountains, to the east the park, and to the south were other apartments, all their lights a Milky Way for the city.

One cool evening, I was on the roof smoking a cigarette when I caught sight of a woman near the north ledge. She stood with her back to me, a snakelike gathering of brown hair to her hips. Silver bracelets like coils choked her wrists, and a sheer blouse, wavering with the wind, clung to her skin. I coughed and she turned around.

"Shit," she said. "I didn't think anyone else came up here."

"Me either," I said and smiled.

We sat on the roof and introduced ourselves. Her name was Monica and she lived by herself on the first floor. There was an elegant gap between her front teeth, and her eyebrows were prominent, high black curves. I told her I was staying with my mother and that I had come from California.

"But you had the beach and all that sunshine."

"Guess it wasn't for me." I pulled my cigarettes from my purse, offering her one.

"Unfiltered Camels," she said. "When my husband was alive, this was his brand."

She looked too young to be a widow, maybe twenty-five at the most.

"Bruce was a drinker all his life," she said. "The only thing he loved more than me. It was cirrhosis. He had been sick for almost two years. It's hard watching someone vanish like that."

I told her that I was sorry. "How long were you married?"

"Six years. All of them right here." Monica stood and tossed her cigarette over the roof. "Glad you came up here tonight."

"Why's that?"

"Because I was going to kill myself. Only the roof didn't seem high enough." Monica walked away and laughed, like the joke was on me.

"What're your plans today?" My mother stood in my doorway, fresh from the shower in a towel and struggling with the clasp on her sterling crucifix necklace. Her hair was still wet, dripping down her collarbones.

"I don't know," I said, sitting up in bed. "Maybe I'll look for jobs." I had enough savings to carry me for a while, though my mother insisted that working wasn't only about money—it was about structure, purpose, keeping track of days.

She set a slip of paper across my quilt. "Groceries. See how much it costs to feed us each week." Tortillas, skim milk, Diet Coke, eggs, coffee, various meats, and many fruits. I pinched the list with two fingers and placed it on my nightstand.

"I'll go when I get some time."

"All you have is time. That's the problem, mija." My mother turned around and reached for something in the hallway. She handed me a small shopping bag. "The salesgirl said it'll cover anything. Burns to rashes. Now you don't have to be ashamed to go outside."

"I'm not ashamed." Inside the bag was a bottle of foundation. I tested the color on my wrist, a perfect match. "No one sees me, anyway. People pretend they don't see a girl with a bruised face."

I left around noon, walking through the park. It was overcast and the breeze carried a slight chill. I went past a homeless man who slept beneath a spruce tree near the pavilion. I saw him most days under the branches with his rootlike hands and ancient face. Today he was crouched over a coverless book, his trash bags of things neatly stacked around his legs. With his eyes to the page, he said, "It's going to rain, miss. Make sure you grab an umbrella." I thanked him and continued across the park.

Several yards ahead, a woman lay on a beach towel in a bikini, her legs halfway bent, their color a natural bronze. Her skin was brilliant with tanning oil and she wore large, Audrey Hepburn sunglasses. As I got closer, I realized it was Monica.

"I know what you're thinking," she said as I stood above her. "Why am I tanning with no sun? It's a great time to be at the park. Everyone's at work. It's empty. Well, not that empty." She lowered her sunglasses and glanced around. "Cheesman used to be a cemetery. Did you know that?"

"No," I said, shaking my head.

"Look around. The land is uneven. The headstones were moved, but hundreds, maybe thousands of bodies were left behind. Mostly the poor, people without family, that kind of thing. They say it's haunted."

"Where did you hear all this?"

Monica removed her sunglasses, revealing hazel eyes and a trickle of freckles. "I just know it. My family's from Colorado. More generations than I can count."

"Me, too, on my mom's side. But my dad was from Detroit."

"Then you know a lot about death and decay." She laughed, rubbing her lean arms, trying to generate warmth. She edged back on her elbows and with her right hand patted the grass, offering me a spot beside her. I shook my head, explaining that I was on my way to get groceries. Then I needed to look for jobs.

"What kind of work?"

"Anything, I guess. I worked at a bank in California, but I didn't like it."

"Not glamorous enough for you?" Monica poked her arms through a beige sweater. "I need help clearing out my apartment. I can't stand to look at my husband's things without crying. I would pay you."

The sky groaned and rain clouds sagged over the city. I imagined the moisture was good for the grass, bones and all. "When would you want me to come over?"

Monica huffed across her sunglasses and cleaned them on her sweater. She checked her reflection in the lenses, sliding her hair from one shoulder to the other. She smiled at herself before putting the sunglasses back on her face. "How about tonight?"


Monica's apartment was long and wide with three bedrooms and a patio covered in thick vines and wicker chairs. Seashell ashtrays littered the end tables and countertops. A steady breeze sent lime-colored drapes fluttering over the hardwood floor. On brick walls were many framed photos of a husky white-haired man in his mid-fifties and his pretty young wife, Monica.

"That's Bruce." Monica pointed to one of the photos. "Always laughing. Always in that stupid leather jacket. I was crazy about him. People thought I was after his money, but I wasn't. He was so kind, Liz. The kindest man I had ever met."

She sighed and headed into the kitchen. I heard her knocking around in the freezer. Ice fell to the floor, a drawer opened, a glass chimed. Then I heard crying. When Monica reappeared with two drinks, her mascara was off her lashes, darkening the high bones surrounding her eyes. She handed me a drink and continued talking.

"He owned the jazz club downtown, the Mermaid Room. We met when I was only nineteen, sneaking in with a fake ID. It wasn't love at first sight, but I grew into him."

"Do you think that's true?" I asked. "Love at first sight."

"Heck yes."

"I met a guy once," I said, hesitantly. "At this tiny bar with overpriced drinks. He teased me about wearing no bra and I made fun of his beaded prayer bracelet. I kept thinking he felt familiar, but also new. I had never wanted someone so quickly. We ended up having sex in his car a few blocks away. I'm pretty sure he had a wife or girlfriend at home. I wanted to cry when it was over."

Monica dropped her gaze, focusing on her drink. The lines of a smirk widened her narrow jaw. "Shit, that's not love. That's someone who needs a car wash."

We didn't pack any boxes that day. We talked and drank into the night. The room grew dark, neither of us switching on a lamp. Monica told me more about Bruce. He had rescued her from a string of meaningless jobs bartending. She didn't have to work anymore. She filled her time with salsa dancing and making altars for the dead, colorful wooden boxes with skulls and yellow flowers. "But since Bruce has been gone, I don't feel like doing much."

Monica went quiet. The skin around her eyes twitched, as though an invisible mosquito drew blood from her eyelids. "I loved him so much, Liz. It's like this chunk of me has been ripped from my body. And if I ever forget he's gone, I hate myself."

I took her in my arms and she dampened my right shoulder with tears. Her skin was warm but her hair, resting against my cheek, was cold. I looked around and realized that I was unable to recall the last time I had spent an afternoon with a girlfriend.

Time didn't feel as long or wasteful in the company of another woman.

At some point, I told her about California, all the details I could remember—his wintergreen soap, the image of his fiancée's blond bobby pins scattered across a burgundy bath mat, the garbled feeling of running my tongue over my broken tooth after he hit me in the face.

Monica lightly walked her fingers along the bridge of my nose. "I could see it beneath your makeup . . . Does it hurt?"

"Yeah. I can barely wash my face."

She pulled back. Her face seemed poreless, covered in mist. "You have two things to look forward to. Someday it won't hurt anymore. And someday he'll be dead."

The following Sunday, I met my mother after Mass. From where I sat on a marble bench outside the cathedral, I watched the brass insignia doors open. People poured in two streams out of the church toward the parking lots. My mother broke away from the crowd, stepping down the white stone steps in her creamy dress and tennis shoes. She squinted at my face before hugging me.

"Nice of you to show up," she said. "Only an hour late."

"Come on, Mama. I'm here for our walk."

Exercise, she believed, would keep my mind off California. It worked for her. She maintained a strict walking schedule, no less than an hour a day. That's how she hardly thought of my father and the violence he put her through.

We crossed Colfax Avenue and passed several blocks of liquor stores and pawnshops. We entered Cheesman through a dead-end street, where a slender path fed into a grass clearing. A dozen or so women and children were there doing yoga. A little girl expertly bent her body in half, her blond ringlets bouncing onto the ground. My mother watched with darting eyes. After some time, she turned to me, asking about Monica, referring to her as that skinny girl from the first floor.

"I'm helping clear out her apartment. She's a widow. Isn't that sad, Mama? Especially for someone so young."

"Imagine if she had lost her husband of fifty years instead. Age has nothing to do with sadness."

We came upon the pavilion, with its high-reaching Greek pillars and airy veranda, where a woman sat on a green sheet, a baby blanket slung over her left shoulder as she nursed an infant. My mother and I watched for a moment. It was a pretty sight, the white marble, the sunlight crisp. Then, from the trees, a black dog with wild eyes came slinking forward.

The nursing woman's hair fell into her face as she cocked her neck from side to side. "Go away," she yelled. "Get out of here." But the dog growled and stepped toward her. The woman twisted to the side and the blanket fell from her shoulder, revealing her baby's hairless head on the edge of her tiny white breast. My mother, quick to react, ran to her, covering her breast and yelling for me to get help with the dog.

The homeless man from beneath the spruce tree had emerged from the branches. He walked past me, hunched over and rickety, his salt-and-pepper hair like a frayed bird's nest. He broke into a sprint through the grass, over the stone steps, and onto the ice-like floor of the pavilion. He hollered as he flung his fists and kicked into the air. The dog's muscular body curved into the shape of a shark's fin as it snarled and snapped. The homeless man held his ground and the animal soon retreated, leaving the veranda silent once more. The woman with the infant thanked my mother, ignoring the homeless man as he retreated, slouched and small, back from where he came.

. . . . . . .

"He's a nice man," I told my mother later as we entered our building's lobby.

"He cares about other people." My mother paused at the elevator doors. "Most men don't know the pleasure."

As we rode the elevator, I studied my mother's face, the corkscrew-shaped scar dangling along her jaw. It had never oc- curred to me, but there was a time before that scar, before my mother knew my father, when her face was still unbroken and she was still young.

Monica and I started in the front room. Bruce had collected antiques—cigar boxes filled with hawk feathers, handheld apache drums, little shoe brushes made of ivory and boar bris- tles. Resting on an end table was a pair of silver pistols with curlicue designs over the grip panels. Monica pointed one at my forehead and pulled the trigger. A bluish flame rose from the barrel.

"Gotcha!" she said. "I love these old lighters."

While we stacked boxes, Monica spoke about Bruce's child- hood. His father was a traveling salesman and his mother was a Valium addict. As for Monica, she didn't know her father and, while she was growing up, her mother often sold their furniture for booze. At one point during her childhood, they had a cardboard box for a kitchen table. Monica would watch cartoons alone for hours on an orange shag carpet. Bruce was the same—he felt parented by spaghetti westerns, the Lone Ranger and Tonto, that sort of thing.

"I always told him Tonto means fool," she said. "He claimed I was too literal."

We soon moved on to the bathroom. In the mirror above the sink, I avoided looking at my face and watched Monica bend over the tub, her spine showing through her T-shirt, a grouping of winglike bones. Her reflection smeared away as I opened the medicine cabinet—jars of Italian cologne, half-used cans of shave gel, a razor flecked with white hair.

We worked together on the drawers near the sink. Among the cotton balls and hairbrushes was a yellow rubber duck, a sailor cap adorning his smiling head. Monica giggled, saying something about Bruce living like a child. She was close enough to my face that I could see the white skin of her scalp. I asked if she and Bruce had ever wanted children.

"No, I was pregnant before. When I was seventeen. I had no money. The guy took off. But the couple that adopted her had a lot of land up in the mountains. I remember that. Seemed like a good place for a little girl to run around."

"Maybe someday she'll come looking for you."

"No, I'm not cut out for motherhood." Monica laughed.

"Where should I take all this?" I pointed to the boxes we had packed.

"To a dumpster. I never want to see any of it again."

I nodded, thinking of the several dumpsters along the park. We carried the boxes down the stairs to the parking lot.

"I have a great idea," Monica said suddenly as we loaded the boxes into my car. "Let's go out tonight. You can see Bruce's old club. We can dance and drink. Maybe flirt a little."

"Can't. I'm having dinner with my mom."

"Perfect. Bring her with you." I frowned, thinking of my mom's response.

"I can try," I said.

That night, I waited until it was full dark. Then I tossed Bruce's things into the dumpster on the park's western edge, working up a sweat and breathing heavily as each box sailed from my arms. The streetlamps made the clear tape covering the boxes shimmer like ribbons of water. When I was back in the car, I caught sight of myself in the rearview mirror. The makeup had sweated off my face. My mouth and nose seemed fused together in a greenish column and the almond-shaped corner of my right eye was plum red. My face, I realized, resembled some gruesome mask.

"What will I do there?" my mother asked. "Everyone will think I'm some old lady." She was at the stove in a terry-cloth bathrobe and moccasin slippers, removing a whining teakettle from the burner. Her hair was pinned behind her ears and her face was covered in shining skin cream.

"You'll have fun. You can have a drink or two. It won't kill you."

My mother shot me a look as if to say it very well might kill her. She filled a mug with steaming water and carried it to the table.

"Please, Mama." I pulled a chair beside her. "You never go out."

"That's not true. I am at the college five days a week. I take my walks. I go to church. I am always out—just not with you or your little friend downstairs." She ran her fingers along the mug's brim. The heat fogged her light pink polish. "Come on, Liz. It's silly."

"I haven't been out at all. I sit here all day. I've done nothing."

"You act like all this is my fault."

I remained silent, running my fingers along the rippled bridge of my nose.

"Oh, fine," she said. "But I won't stay long."

—

The Mermaid Room had a low stucco ceiling, an elevated square stage, and a black-and-white checkered floor. Onstage, a sad girl in a satiny dress, a purple iris pinned to her hair, sang into a microphone. *Stormy weather,* she sang syrupy and sweet. *Since my man and I ain't together.*

Monica was in a back booth, leaning over a clear drink with a lime. She wore a slinky sequin top that showed the notches in her rib cage between her breasts. Her eyes were closed and she nodded, humming and swaying to the music. She didn't look up as my mother and I scooted across from her and flung our purses into the booth's corner.

"Damn," Monica said. "How does someone so young know about so much pain?"

"She must pay attention to life," said my mother.

Monica opened her eyes, grinned. "You made it, Mama Liz."

We ordered a round of drinks, my mother sticking to red wine as Monica and I sipped tequila. Monica wasn't her normal chatty self, so I asked what year the building was built, how long Bruce had owned it, where the band was from, if she could sing.

"Oh God, no. I'd bust someone's eardrums."

"She can sing." I lifted my drink toward my mother. "Can't you, Mama?"

"Not like this girl. Not in a million years."

My mother adjusted the collar on her chiffon shirt, centering her crucifix necklace above her sternum, covering a black mole. Her gaze was on the singer, whose dress had a liquid sparkle that turned blinding when she twisted her body toward the right light. The bar erupted with applause as she exited the stage. She curtsied to the left, moving in a milky blur toward the bar. A quartet began setting up.

Monica shuffled through her purse, pulling out a pack of cigarettes. "Care to join?" she asked, and I nodded.

I stood on the sidewalk with Monica, smoking and listening to her talk about a bartender she used to date. "God," she said. "And he always wanted me to be on top. Like it was the fucking Olympics." I laughed and blew smoke toward the bar. I could see my mother through the windows. She remained in the booth, resting her head against the cool wall, her dark hair spreading into shadows. She slowly sipped her wine, keeping her face to the table when a man in a fedora approached her. She tore a napkin to pieces and shook her head.

"Can you believe that singer?" Monica asked. "Will you stay for her second set?"

I told her I couldn't, that I needed to get my mother home. We finished our cigarettes, and when Monica opened the door, music fell into the street. In the distance, a storm gathered beyond the city, thin veins of lightning illuminating the sky.

That night the pelting sounds of rain covered my mother's snoring. I imagined her in the next room, her body a breathing lump beneath a white quilt. For the first time since I had come home, I thought of how lonely she must be. Each day she focused on tasks instead of herself. I wondered if she had ever tried to date a man from the college, a divorced professor perhaps.

I rolled onto my side and fell asleep, where I dreamed of my father. *I'm going ice fishing,* he said. I told him I loved the ice houses. He kissed my forehead and I felt his shape, solid and stifling. He brought me to the lake. We carved a hole into the ice, and he reached inside the black water until he was snagged like a fish caught on a hook. The hole grew larger as he screamed and I feared that when it was done with him, that darkness was coming for me. That's when I woke up and looked at my phone. 3:17 A.M. I had five missed calls, all from Monica.

She was outside our lobby in her white SUV with tinted windows and leather seats. Monica kept the motor running as I got inside. "Let's go for a drive."

I shook rain from my hair. "My mom might wake up and get scared if I'm gone."

"It's not like you sleep in her bed. How will she know you're not there?"

"I'm her child," I said.

Monica drove us down narrow one-way roads, weaving in and out of alleys. The rain fell in slanted white lines. The radio was low on an AM station—someone was talking to someone else about bees and honey. There were hardly any headlights on the road.

"Did you have fun tonight?" Monica asked.

"Bruce's old bar is cool. I like the vibe."

"It never changes. Different bands play, different girls sing, but it always feels like home."

Monica turned off the main road and stopped the SUV. Her headlights beamed outward until they fell upon a set of stone pillars. We were in the lot beside the park's pavilion.

"You know, he chased me for years." Monica lit a cigarette. The flame cast upward shadows on her face. "I used to make fun of him. I told people he was just some old pervert."

She rolled down the window, exhaling smoke in a hurried

line. Her slinky top darkened as rain fell sideways onto her arms and legs, some of it making its way onto my face—the unmistakable warmth of Colorado rain in summer.

"Once we were together, I hoped people realized it was about love. Not that other stuff, money or convenience."

I asked her what people she was talking about. She carried on without an answer.

"He wanted a baby. *Give me a little girl,* he'd say. I heard him crying in the shower about it. This huge man, beneath that running water, crying. And now that he's gone—" Monica faced me. She raised her voice and it broke. "I only want him back."

Between the low chatter on the radio and the constant thumping of rain, it was easy to remain silent as Monica began to cry. Her profile was sharply lit by little lights inside the car. She seemed calm despite the tears rolling off her jaw and into her chest. In that chaos, the heavy fog of breathing, the sounds of a storm, I saw Monica check her reflection in the rearview mirror. From beneath her seat, Monica then handed me a flask and told me to drink. I could be anyone, I thought, and she would still say these things. Monica didn't want help or comfort. She wanted to be seen.

"Take me back home," I said, raising my voice. "My mom will worry."

Monica continued sobbing, throwing her arms around, waving to nobody. Beyond the fogged windows, I stared into the black spaces between the stone pillars. I wanted to go home and crawl into bed. I wanted to wake up and see my mother off before she left for work. We'd have black coffee with fried eggs. She'd encourage me to get out of the house, leaving an umbrella for me in case I decided to walk.

That's when I saw the man. On the curb before the stone pavilion, his head was slumped and he appeared to be sleeping upright in a shiny leather jacket.

"That guy," I said, pointing to the windshield. "He shouldn't be out here in the rain."

"What guy?" she asked, and when I pointed again, Monica opened the door and, with me following her, ran through the rain.

We were a few steps away when I realized it was the homeless man. He was sitting on the sidewalk with a fifth of whiskey, water drizzling down the grooves of his wrinkles. When he saw us approaching, he smiled deliriously and lifted the half-empty bottle. "A swig," he said, "for you, the beautiful ladies."

Monica was stunned, like she was seeing a ghost, but it was the image of someone else in her dead husband's jacket. She knocked the whiskey from the homeless man's hand, breaking the bottle at my feet, the amber-colored liquid instantly swallowed by the sidewalk and the early morning rain.

"We don't need roughhousing," the homeless man said. "You wasteful girl."

Monica yanked his left arm. "This is my husband's jacket."

The homeless man said nothing. He opened and closed a fist, as though muscle memory was forcing him to reach for the bottle.

"You dug it out of the trash," Monica yelled. "Didn't you? Like a dog."

The homeless man frowned, muttering something about being thirsty, and Monica grabbed a fistful of his hair. He let out a howl. "Stop, miss, please. I wasn't causing you harm."

Monica's face relaxed as something went blank in her eyes. It was a look I had seen countless times in my father's face. Monica jerked the homeless man's neck with both hands. She toppled him onto his side, letting out the dull boom of a body on concrete. With the tip of her pointed heel, she kicked him in the gut, the face, anywhere she could. The homeless man wailed in agony.

Monica lifted her leg to kick him once more, but I kneeled beside him to block her blows. Her foot lodged itself into the small of my back, sending me forward until my face was an inch from the homeless man's. He was crying, the grooves in his face drenched with rain. I pleaded for Monica to stop.

"I gave it to him," I said. "I saw him at night without a coat. I had the boxes in my car. I wanted him to be warm."

Monica paused her kicking. The homeless man removed one arm from the jacket's sleeve and then the other, tossing the coat onto the curb, where it rested like a dog's tongue. He shivered in a sodden flannel, soaked to his skin. I leaned down to him and whispered soothing lies that everything would be all right. The homeless man looked at my face, his eyes webbed in bloody veins.

"Someone hurt you," he said. "They hurt you bad."

I walked home in the rain and stayed in the shower for a long time. Wrapped in a towel, I leaned in the doorway of my mother's bedroom. Silently crying, I watched as she slept.

Not long before I left California, my mother called just to chat.

"I've been looking at some photos of myself," she said. "Mostly from when I was with your father. I'm a little embarrassed."

"Why's that?"

"I can tell how sad I look. It's something in my eyes. There's this dull light inside them. I'm starting to wonder if it's always been there. If I looked that way before your father, when I was a teenager, or even a little girl."

"You just have dark eyes," I said. "Plenty of people do. I know I do."

"No, it's different. What happened to me that made me look so sad?" She laughed and I heard her sipping from a glass. "I get embarrassed. I kept wondering how many people recognized that sadness in me. Probably more than I'd like to know. But it changed."

I asked her how, pulling the phone a little away from my ear, holding up a finger, and letting the man in my bed know it wouldn't be much longer.

"The world did. It became less urgent, somehow bigger, and I didn't worry so much about being loved."

# TOMI

· · · · · · · · · · · · · · · · ·

When my nephew Tomi was a baby, I stole the thousand
dollars his mother, Natalie, kept in her closet. It was for
his college fund. She had placed the money in a rinsed-out mason
jar, wrapped in a knockoff Fendi scarf and hidden beneath a pile
of balled socks. Hungover and dazed, I crept across their carpeted floor, taking the jar and spending everything on liquor and
clothes within a week. Natalie always suspected it was me,
though Manny said I would never do something like that.
"Who," he demanded, "would steal from their own blood?"

Six years later, I stole a '94 Honda Civic and drove head-on
into an elderly couple's picture window at four in the morning.
It was in the northern suburbs. Every house and driveway
looked like a white gravel road. An old man wore striped pajamas as he dusted shattered windshield glass from my face.
Blood flooded my mouth. A tooth dragged down my throat.
The old man placed a towel on my lips and told his wife to call
an ambulance. When he leaned back through the car door, his

pajama arm resting on the steering wheel, he said, "Look at you, jita. You're just a baby."

I served my time at La Vista Correctional Facility in Pueblo, Colorado. My family didn't call much and they never visited. I marked the days on two calendars—the first filled with illustrations of wildflowers and the second with photos of horses in empty rustic fields. Toward the end of the horses, my attorney wrote to say that I was up for early release, so long as I had a place to live and I got a job. I planned on moving into a halfway house off Colfax Avenue when Manny called to say I could live with him and Tomi.

"Won't Natalie be pissed?" I asked Manny over the phone.

"She's gone. She left me."

I told him I was sorry, even though I had seen it coming. At seventeen, Natalie had moved into our house with only a snap-close suitcase, two Navajo blankets, and her belly full of Tomi.

"Why are you doing this?" I asked Manny before hanging up.

"You're my sister, Cole, my blood. But please don't fuck up this time."

When he was twenty-one and I was fifteen, Manny inherited our family home after our father died of a heart attack while shampooing his hair. Our mother was already long dead. When I was very little she swallowed an entire bottle of painkillers. At La Vista, I read in an anatomy book that the heart has no nerve endings and for a little while, I believed my parents died without any pain. We lived on Denver's Northside, in the shadow of Mile High Stadium, a neighborhood that was now called Highlands, though only white people said that. Our house was a slender brick square that rested on a high plot, giving it the illusion of something great among knifing condos and black

BMWs. The gentrification reminded me of tornadoes, demolishing one block while casually leaving another intact. Our block, Vallejo Street, was unrecognizable.

I was released from La Vista early on a Tuesday morning in late autumn. Manny met me outside in his white Tacoma that reeked of corn chips and coffee. He wore his canvas Carhartt, his dark hair newly streaked white.

"Look at you," he said, pinching my cheeks. "Someone called Jenny Craig."

"Yeah, prison don't have any Bud Light."

"Damn shame. I'll get you some chicharrones for the road."

He turned up the radio on a Neil Young song and beat out the chorus on the steering wheel. A red rosary dangled snake-like from the rearview mirror. Taped to the dash were Virgin of Guadalupe prayer cards and a Sears baby picture of Tomi.

"How is he?" I asked, brushing the photo with my hand. "Since Natalie's been gone."

"I don't know. Sad." Manny pinched tobacco into his left cheek. "He's failing a class called Read and Relax. You tell me how a person fails to read and relax."

We drove by a yellow traffic sign, bullet-holed and bent, warning against picking up hitchhikers when near a correctional facility. The sky beyond was larger than I'd ever seen, an oily gray with arrowheads of birds.

"Impressive," I said.

Manny parked the Tacoma outside our house. I pointed to a glass high-rise that had appeared where a vacant warehouse once stood. It reflected the clouds, the winged tips of the mountains. "That's pretty fancy," I said.

"Yeah, real fancy. It also ruins my view of the stadium. These property taxes are fucking me," said Manny. "But we were here first. I'll be damned before I move to the suburbs."

Inside, Tomi was on the living room floor, his hair a mop of black strands. He clutched a videogame controller, swaying right and left, forward and back. His glasses were smudged with spotted fingerprints, reflecting the sparkling blue lights of the television.

Manny hung his Broncos hat on the rack and unzipped his Carhartt. He had grown softer around his middle and I wondered if I looked older, too. "Get up," he said. "Say hi to your auntie."

Tomi flung forward. Videogame blood splattered the screen. "Hi to your auntie."

"Ay." Manny walked over, swatting Tomi's head with his right palm. "Don't act like such a shithead. She's traveled a long way, Son."

Tomi looked at me, squinting with sarcasm. "Why hello, Auntie Nicole."

"Just call me Cole, Tomi. Really."

Manny showed me to the windowless basement where I had stayed before La Vista. Everything was the same as when I left. The stench of mothballs, the hanging lightbulb, my faded size 16 jeans stuffed into a cardboard box. I spotted my Kmart futon with a busted seam and Manny gave the white aluminum frame a good shake. "It won't be too comfortable. There aren't any pillows."

"Why not?"

"I think Natalie took them. I've looked everywhere. Tomi and I slept with our heads on folded towels last night. I shit you not, towels."

"That's child abuse. Even the prison had pillows. Get some new ones."

"It's the principle of the thing. Natalie thinks she can take off like that, stealing sheets and pillows and whatever else I can't find around here."

I nodded and looked past him, studying a rippling crack in the cement wall. The room was as big as four cells at La Vista, maybe five. "I gotta nap."

"I need to head back to the office, anyway." Manny handed me two stolen hotel towels for pillows and told me to enjoy.

I woke up a couple hours later to the sounds of gunshots. Tomi was in the same position as before, seated on a leather sofa cushion like a little Buddha. On the television screen, things were being blown up. He kept his eyes to the TV when I said hello. "You woke me up, dude. I was trying to take a nap."

Tomi lurched forward with his videogame controller, his mouth shiny with spit.

"So, you're pretty big now," I said. This was an understatement. He was the heaviest little kid I'd ever seen. "What're you playing?"

"Call of Duty."

"What's that?"

He glared at me. "You're not like how I remember. You were fat."

"I was fat? You sure you know what fat looks like?"

He paused his game and twisted around to face me. "You were, like, a fat goth chick or something."

"People change. Anyway, I was sleeping. Maybe turn down the volume or read a book. Quiet kid things."

Tomi rose from the cushion. I watched him walk to the kitchen in mismatched socks and oversize pipe shorts. He grabbed a carton of Sunny Delight from the fridge. He poured a glass, got himself some Gushers from the pantry, and returned to his seat. He unpaused his game and blew up a helicopter.

"You shouldn't be sleeping at three in the afternoon," he said. "Only bums do that."

The next morning, I called my parole officer from Manny's house phone. She was an older woman from Nebraska named Charlie Mae and spoke with a slight lisp.

"Now, Nicole, you need to start making some job contacts."

"I've been home a day."

"That's no excuse. It's already noon."

"I'm not qualified for much."

"Sure you are," she said. "Find your niche. That thing you like."

At La Vista, I had taken enrichment classes. Some lady from the community college taught us how to make traditional Pueblo Indian pinch pots. Another woman visited with notebooks filled with nature sketches and tracings of dead birds. The class I liked most, though, was Language Arts. We read *Lilies of the Field* and I had this clear picture of a little desert town. I liked going there, so I read the book more than once. I also loved biographies, especially about women inventors, like Bette Graham, who came up with white-out. I thought maybe I could do something like that—come up with my own inventions, but after I got out, I knew no one would have enough faith in me.

That afternoon I walked three blocks to Thirty-second Avenue. Blond women with high ponytails pushed babies in expensive strollers while white guys in khakis stared at their cellphones, sidestepping fallen leaves. I went into a tea shop that had once been a liquor store and handed the frizzy-haired redhead my résumé. She wore beaded earrings and colorful New Age crystals around her neck.

"You have experience with teas?" she asked, her eyes looking out from delicate, wire-framed glasses.

"Oh yes," I said. "I can steep the shit out of a tea bag."

She stared at me and cleared her throat. "We're not hiring."

I was back at Manny's, sitting in front of the empty fireplace, drinking a cup of chamomile tea in place of beer, when Tomi came home. Without noticing me, he stepped into the kitchen wearing earbuds. He opened the refrigerator, grabbed the Sunny Delight, tipped his head back, and guzzled.

I gently yanked his earbuds. "Shouldn't you be at school?"

He wiped his juice mustache on the back of his hand. "Shouldn't you be out getting a job?"

"For your information, I was out looking for jobs earlier." I grabbed the bottle of Sunny Delight. "This is gross. You know how many calories this has? Your dad shouldn't buy this. It's sugar water."

"Whatever. You should know. You used to be a fat goth cokehead."

I opened my mouth and lowered my eyebrows, pretending to be offended. Tomi didn't flinch. His little freckled moon face remained fixed in an angry scowl.

I flicked his backpack strap and flung my index finger into the air.

"Let's get something straight, Tomás Manuel Morales. One, I was not goth. I just liked purple lip liner. Two, I wasn't *that* fat. And three, I wasn't a cokehead. If I was, I would have been skinny. Everybody knows that."

Tomi scrunched his face. A deep line formed between his eyebrows.

"Are you going to make me go back to school?"

———

"Do you think he plays videogames too much?" I asked Manny as he dug through the hallway closet, searching for a set of sheets. After tossing into the corner several pillow covers that our mother had crocheted, he stepped away from the shelves. There was a dusty cinnamon smell like our mother's hair, though it must have been a memory, something tricking my mind.

"Christ almighty," Manny said, his face hidden by the bill of a Rockies hat, the slight shadow spreading down his flannel shirt like a bib.

It was Saturday. That meant working around the house for Manny and nothing else. He removed his hat. He wiped sweat with his shirtsleeve from his forehead. He muttered something about Natalie taking the pillows and God knows what else. He then placed his hands on his lower back, letting out a groan.

"Tomi is dealing with a lot right now. If it makes him happy to play some videogames, I'm not going to take away his happiness. Let the boy be."

"Does she even see him?" I asked.

Manny rubbed the stubble on his neck. He walked across the hallway until he stood beneath the attic door, unlooping its roped latch from its resting place. "No."

"Honestly, I never liked Natalie. She's a selfish bitch." The truth was, in the beginning, I wanted to like her, I wanted her to be the sister I never had. But Natalie scared me. It wasn't unusual for her to fight when we were younger. She once shattered a dish across Manny's face when he'd embarrassed her at a cousin's birthday party.

Manny pried open the attic. There was a cool and anxious draft. "Don't call my son's mother a bitch."

· · · · · · ·

"Some mother," I said, gathering the pillow covers from the floor and placing them back in the closet. That's when I caught sight of Manny's bedroom down the hallway, the door halfway open revealing his unmade pillowless bed. It was strange not having Natalie in the house. I once saw her on the edge of that bed, crying with strands of her black ponytail caught in her mouth. "You think this is what I want, Cole?" she had asked when our eyes met. She was eight months pregnant with Tomi and as she walked out of my sight, she resembled a little girl with a balloon tucked underneath her shirt, playing pretend.

"I mean it about Tomi," I said after some time. "It isn't right for a kid to sit inside all day. He should be out building a fort or finding dead bodies in the woods. You know, like in *Stand by Me.*"

Manny started up the wooden ladder, his torso disappearing into the skull of the house. "Worry about getting yourself a job."

Tomi was on the sofa cushion, clicking the remote and staring at the blank TV screen. I sat on a recliner pretending not to notice anything unusual. While he was at school, I had unplugged some cables from the wall. I hid them behind the elliptical in the basement, the one place he'd never look.

Tomi walked to the TV, pushed some more buttons, and said, "Where are they?"

"I heard your mom jacked the pillows. Why don't you ask her ass?"

Tomi looked defeated. He slumped forward and stared at his mismatched socks, wiggling a toe through a tiny hole. He wore a black T-shirt with flames and traced his plump index finger over the printed fire. "She's such a bad person."

"All moms are crazy," I told him. "I was about to go to the bookstore. Come with me?"

Tomi twisted his face while tapping his socked foot against the carpet. He threw his head around and rolled his eyes beneath his glasses.

"Don't start convulsing," I said.

"Whatever."

"Do you want to go to the bookstore or not?"

"I can't believe you like to read," said Tomi.

"I was in prison. What do you think I did all day?"


Tomi walked like a little boy lost in a world of wonder. I was stunned by how, at the edge of a pond, he reached up and gently held the dying leaf of a tree. It had rained earlier. Clear beads of moisture clung to the branch. He snapped the leaf from its stem. Leftover water pelted our heads as Tomi threw the leaf to the sidewalk, crushing it with his enormous padded tennis shoes.

"Did your mom ever take you on walks?" I asked.

"We used to," Tomi said. "We'd go with Dad in the summer, before the sun went down."

"I used to walk with my mom, too."

"Grandma Louise?"

I nodded. "Did your dad tell you about her?"

"Yup. He said she made really pretty blankets."

I smiled. I told Tomi that was true.

"Hey, Cole, which room was yours growing up? Was it mine or the other one, the big room with the bathroom connected?"

He was talking about the master bedroom, where my father had collapsed in the shower. It's also where my mother fell asleep when I was eight years old and never woke up. No one stayed in that room anymore. There were too many ghosts.

Manny used the room as storage, filled it with Christmas decorations, Tomi's old baby bassinet, seasonal junk.

"I had your room," I said. "Watch out, there might be goth crap hidden in the floorboards."

Tomi snickered. "Our room sucks. The big tree in the front yard blocks my view of everything."

"It's not too bad." I thought of how I used to climb down from my window and onto that cottonwood tree as a teenager, bottles of stolen tequila and a few stray beers in my backpack. My getaway tree.

Tomi strolled ahead, his jeans making jingling noises, as if he were a janitor carrying around keys to a thousand rooms. "It's the worst. When my mom left, I couldn't see her at all. I could hear her car and all that, but I couldn't see anything but those stupid leaves."

"Where's your mom now?"

"She's with her new boyfriend, Ronald. She tried to take me over there, but I hated it. He smells like a ferret and he's really into Frisbee golf."

"That's really weird."

"It is really fucking weird."

"Watch it." I lightly slapped the back of his head. "Don't cuss."

At the bookstore, I showed Tomi the teen section, an overflowing back corner with a dirty love seat. There were posters on the walls of nineties celebrities posing with copies of *Beloved* and *Moby-Dick*.

"See," I told him. "Even Buffy the Vampire Slayer likes to read."

When he asked who that was, I said never mind and told him to pick out a book. I walked to the entrance and thought of asking the clerk for an application, but I knew this wasn't the sort of place where they'd hire an ex-convict.

After a little while, Tomi tapped my shoulder and presented me with a book. The cover image was of an exceptionally suntanned warrior descending a volcano as he thrust the bloody heart of a sacrificial victim into the air. Behind him, a bolt of white lightning illuminated the title, *Azteca Moonrise*. "It's a whole series," Tomi whispered. "How many can I get?"

I was released from prison with two hundred bucks and some change.

"How about you get Book One. If you like it, we'll come back for the second."

"Nice. These books look badass." Tomi sent the pages fluttering with his thumb. "Hey, Cole. I'm not retarded or anything."

"I never said you were."

"I know, but sometimes I get mixed up on words. My mom used to help, but she's busy playing Frisbee golf now."

"That sucks. You want my help?"

The next day after school, Tomi sat beside me at the kitchen table, his fleshy arms folded beneath his chin, *Azteca Moonrise* in front of us. We stayed for an hour, our necks bent over the pages aching from marathon reading and sleeping without pillows. Tomi, I discovered, was a slow reader, to the point that it worried me. Over the next few days I researched reading strategies online. Visualization. Annotating. We tried them out and within a couple weeks, Tomi actually showed improvement. He especially loved reading aloud. Whenever he got to a passage with a warrior sacrificing a virgin, Tomi passed the book to me.

"I like how you do the voices," he'd say, and I always thanked him, reminding him that I played Rudolph in the La Vista Christmas pageant, two years running.

—

A few weeks after Tomi and I started reading *Azteca Moonrise*, Manny came home with a paper grocery sack and two shot glasses. He sat at the kitchen table and let out a drafty sigh. I curled my arm around the sofa's back to face him. From the paper sack, he pulled out a bottle of Hornitos and set it on the table with a clink. Manny twirled the bottle by its long neck, smirked. "Got a sales bonus today. Five hundred bones."

"Congratulations. Now get that shit out of here."

"What are the chances your PO will show?"

I glared at Manny. "As good a chance as any other night. Take it out to your truck."

I reminded him that as part of my early release, Charlie Mae could visit whenever she pleased. I could hear her voice saying, *No alcohol or other forms of contraband allowed in the domicile.* I could go back to La Vista for a thimble of marshmallow-flavored vodka.

Manny moved his hand around the tequila's top, as though he were unscrewing its cap. With the bottle still sealed, he poured imaginary shots. He licked the back of his left hand, dashed out some salt. "Arriba, abajo."

"You're crazy," I said and joined him at the table.

The bonus had nothing to do with Manny's desire to drink real or imagined liquor. He was in a wistful mood, reminiscing, talking about our parents and telling stories from back in the day. "You were so damn scared," he kept saying about the time I fell from the cottonwood tree that my father had warned us against. *One wrong move and you kids will break your necks.* Manny had rushed barefoot into the front yard, slicing open his heel on a broken bottle someone had tossed onto our lawn. As he carried me inside, he left bloody footprints on the hardwood floor. I looked over his shoulder at the shining red pools. "Is it my neck?" I asked. "No," he said. "It's mine."

"I'm worried about Tomi," I told Manny after some time. "I think he has a problem. A reading problem."

"He's eleven and doesn't like to read. It's normal."

"Ten," I said.

"What?"

"Ten. Tomi is ten."

I studied Manny's face and wondered if he resembled our father at that age. Long lines trailed from the sides of his nose down to the edges of his mouth. His dark eyes were bright, though heavy with bags. At La Vista, I often pictured Manny as a little boy, his grave face and stern eyes, but he was never a child to me, always the big brother, always the grown-up.

"Why didn't you visit me?" I said.

Manny dropped his gaze to his lap. "Natalie didn't want to go. Said it wouldn't be good for Tomi."

"I needed you," I said softly.

"I didn't want to see you in a place like that. What do you want me to say?"

"That you're sorry."

Manny shook his head and poured another make-believe shot. He raised it to me. "I swear on our parents' lives, if you ever drive a stolen vehicle while under the influence into a residential building again, I will visit you in prison."

I swallowed, attempting to calm my trembling throat. "Shut up, asshole."

Tomi and I finished *Azteca Moonrise* on a Wednesday afternoon. We read the final page out loud together, and after the last line, Tomi looked at me, almost tearful, and said, "*Azteca*

*Starship* awaits." He pushed his glasses up the bridge of his nose. "Let's go to the bookstore right now." I didn't have any cash left, and while I thought to ask Manny for help, I knew he'd just tell me to get a job.

"Let's try the library? We can take the bus. Every ride is an adventure."

"Yeah," Tomi said. "For poor people."

"Well, I'm poor. And you're ten. That makes you poor by default."

The bus drove through a part of downtown where new metallic apartments jutted into the skyline, mimicking the view of the mountains. Traffic swarmed and coughed under the city's haze and healthy looking young people rode bikes through the streets, past the homeless who curled under wilted cardboard. Tomi sat beside me, looking out the window. As we neared the library, he leaned over me like a puppy about to pee.

"See that house?" he asked, pointing enthusiastically at a newly remodeled bungalow. "I think that's Ronald's house. Where my mom lives now."

I stared at the house, trying to imagine Natalie in a home like that. It didn't seem plausible. It had a clean, square lawn and in place of an ancient cottonwood, infant trees were held upright with tiny ropes. The house even had a three-car garage and a basketball hoop beneath an American flag. "I don't think she lives there," I said. "Your mom wouldn't like a home like that." But as the bus rounded the corner, Natalie's Honda pulled into the driveway and we both grew quiet.

At the central library, a security guard beneath a string of enormous Colorado flags greeted us. The wide space was cool with marble floors. Tomi flicked my purse strap as I searched the database for *Azteca Starship*. We learned from the back of Book One that this volume included a sacrifice in space. We both had many questions, like where does blood spurt in zero gravity and are jaguar teeth and obsidian spikes still the preferred weapons? I wrote the author's name on a white square of paper and told Tomi to follow me. We zigzagged in and out of aisles, our chins tilted upward until we eventually stood before our shelf, the whole of the Azteca Intergalactic Series before us.

"I don't understand," I said, looking at my paper. "It should be right here."

Tomi jumped to see higher. "It's not?"

"No, it's missing."

"This sucks," said Tomi. "Of course it's gone." He kicked the shelf, his puffy shoe sliding off, exposing his white sock. His dark eyes were fixed on a certain point and it appeared he was searching the bookshelf behind me, but he wasn't.

He looked directly at my face. "Cole, what happened to your tooth?"

"Excuse me?"

"Your tooth." Tomi pointed to my mouth. "I saw it was gone when we were reading. I didn't want to say anything. My mom says I should ignore things like that."

The last person to say anything about my tooth was the dentist at La Vista, who told me he could replace it. *Might as well take advantage of free dental,* he had said. I felt inside my mouth, the black space of my long-gone molar. "I swallowed it. When I crashed a car."

"That car you stole?"

I nodded.

"Why did you do that?"

"I don't know. I used to drink a lot, but I'm not that way anymore."

Tomi turned his face to the side, bowing his head like he suddenly understood something very important. He seemed worn down, old beyond his years. He almost looked like Manny.

"My mom told me you stole from me."

"Yeah," I heard myself say. "I did that, too." I searched the bookshelf, everything an endless line of colorful spines. When I looked back at Tomi, his face had shifted, his dark brown eyes suddenly appearing far away. "Stay here," I said. "I'll ask a librarian."

I waited in line for the reference librarian, an older Chicano with a heft of gold around his neck. He had porcupine hair the color of burnt firewood. When I finally reached his desk, he told me *Azteca Starship* was nowhere to be found. He then pushed up his shirtsleeves and waved a coverless book in my face. "You'll like this one better. Have you read it?"

"I don't know what that is," I said.

"Probably because you're too young. It's a great one, jita."

I walked away from him and peered down the aisle where Tomi had been. He was gone. I called back to the librarian. "I was with a little boy. My nephew. Have you seen him?"

The librarian shrugged. "Prunes."

"*What?*"

"Maybe he needed to use the shitter?"

"No," I said, nervously. "He was just here."

The librarian laughed from his gut. "Back in a flash."

After I watched him calmly walk to the front desk, I searched for Tomi in the kids' books, the archival stacks, and the empty men's bathroom. "Tomi," I kept saying until my voice became a frantic yell. I checked outside around a brass statue of children holding hands and ran over to the picnic tables along the parking lot. But he was nowhere. Had he run away or been kidnapped? I pictured Tomi clumsily climbing into a stranger's white van, an armful of Twizzlers as bait. Panic had set in, my heartbeat riding my veins. "Tomi," I screamed. "Please come back."

The librarian had come outside with a security guard and both men had the stiffened posture of those delivering bad news. I approached them, and the librarian placed his right hand on my shoulder. "Bad news, Rik here thinks he saw him leave."

"Leave," I said. "Leave where?"

"How did you lose him?" the security guard asked.

"Lose him? No, he was just here. His name's Tomi and he's eleven. Ten. I mean ten. He has dark brown hair and glasses, and these big shoes." I felt something like hiccups in my chest. "He's too little to be alone."

The librarian and security guard shared a look. It wasn't good.

"Can you think of anywhere he'd go? A friend's house or a park?"

"It's nighttime. He doesn't know anything."

"Ma'am," the security guard said, "have you been drinking?"

"Are you serious?"

He said, "I've seen you before. I know how you Northside girls are."

"Ay, come now," said the librarian. "She doesn't seem *too* messed up."

People coming out of the library had turned to look at us. A slim woman in pink spandex, holding her toddler on her hip, spun around so that her daughter faced the brick wall. That's when I knew where Tomi had gone.

"That wasn't me," I said. "You must have me confused with someone else."

———

There was a night a long time ago when I didn't drive myself home wasted from a party. I sat in a cab's passenger seat, marveling at the ribbons of green and blue city lights. It could have been the haze of weed, the heaviness of liquor, but I felt submerged, as if I had finally gotten to the real city, the ground floor, the place where everything is born. I asked my driver what was the strangest place in Denver he'd seen, the worst area. I thought he'd say my neighborhood, before it changed, but he didn't. He said, "Cherry Hills, all them mansions give me the creeps. It's like the entire neighborhood, the whole city, died in its sleep." That's how I felt as I stood on Natalie's new white porch, and equally ashamed and afraid at the sight of Manny's truck out front. I knocked hard on the door.

A middle-aged white woman answered in hiking clothes. She kept the chain on as she spoke. "Can I help you?"

I told her that I was looking for Natalie. Natalie Morales.

"She said her name is something else. Durán?"

"It used to be that. Is she here?"

The woman unlatched the chain. She stepped out of the house with a flood of warmth. "Natalie's in the back. She and Ron rent my guesthouse." She directed me to a sandstone path where small lamps illuminated the way. "How nice she has visitors," she said with disdain.

Manny and Natalie were in the backyard between the two houses, shouting in clipped tones above the dark grass. Tomi sat in a plastic chair on the guesthouse stoop, a gangly white guy beside him, watching over the altercation like some shitty owl.

*Ronald*, I thought. *What a catch.*

When Tomi saw me, he removed his glasses, setting them in his lap. Natalie sharked around, her long hair, lightened to a caramel color, waved across the yard. She stood before me, looking small and silly with her blondish hair. She'd lost weight, too, like she wore her skeleton over her skin.

"Her," Natalie screamed at Manny, pointing in my direction. "You let some ex-con watch Tomi." She turned to me then, her eyes glinting with rage. "You're a worthless piece of shit, Nicole. Do not take my son anywhere again."

I started laughing. "Where would I take him? To visit you?"

Behind us, the lights of the big house flipped on, and there were sounds like someone stumbling down a staircase. Ronald sipped a beer covered in a koozie. "Babe, babe, let's be more respectful to Shauna," he said.

I gazed at Natalie. "You left to live here with your ugly-ass boyfriend who smells like a ferret?"

Natalie reached up and popped me in the mouth. Blood spurted from my bottom lip. I wiped the red on my hands, searching for somewhere to spit the iron taste. I saw her herb garden, planted neatly beneath sheer umbrellas. I walked over, kicked aside the plastic cover, and coughed blood all over her dead rosemary.

"You hit her," I heard Tomi shout.

I looked at him and saw how scared and sad and small he was. His glasses were back on his face, magnifying his brown eyes. In his lap, he roped his hands over his tummy. I immediately felt worse for being there. What kind of people were we? Tomi had watched his aunt fight his mother in the yard of a guesthouse she shared with some idiot who owned a koozie. His father was standing by, mortified, face-to-face with his wife's new white boyfriend.

"If you touch me," Natalie screamed, "I'll call the police and you'll be back where you belong."

"We're leaving," Manny said, marching over and gripping Tomi's forearm.

As we headed for the pickup, Manny turned back and asked, politely as possible, for the pillows. Natalie ignored him and slammed shut the guesthouse door. I felt sorry for her then. I knew she was embarrassed by herself, and had been her whole life. She'd always feel like that brown girl from the Northside with a baby at seventeen, living in her husband's decrepit house. I thought of something my father used to say in Spanish, *You cannot straighten the trunk of a crooked tree.*

At home, Tomi ran to his bedroom while Manny went into the kitchen and filled a glass of water. He handed it to me and sat at the table, motioning for me to do the same.

"What happened?" I asked.

"He just walked over there," Manny said. "He misses his mom, I guess."

"Was he scared? Did he get lost?"

"He's fine, but you can't do something like that again. You need to watch him better."

I told him that it was an accident, that Tomi took off on his own. But the more I spoke, the more painfully familiar my voice sounded, like a recording of myself from years ago.

I paused, listening to the house sounds instead. The refrigerator buzzed. The floorboards creaked. It was like our home was an old man with a damp cough.

"I think there's something wrong with me," I said.

"Your reflexes could use some help. Duck next time."

"No, like as a person." I couldn't hold back from crying.

Tears flowed down my nose, salting my split lip. "I always screw up. I always hurt my family."

Manny looked around, searching for napkins, finding none. With quick fingers, he unbuttoned his flannel, placing it in my hands.

"Wipe off your face. There's nothing wrong with you. And there never was." He stood from his seat, starting up the stairs with an arched back, looking oddly thin in his white undershirt.

"Tomorrow I'm going to help you look for jobs. We'll start early. Make sure you're awake." Manny quieted his voice. "I'm sorry that I didn't visit you, Cole."

"Thank you, Brother."

"You're a lot better than you used to be. A lot better."

After he went upstairs to bed, the house was silent. I stayed at the table for a long while, thinking about many things, my mother and father, my brother and myself as children, how black Manny's hair had once been, how little our home had changed. The ancient oak floors, the strange dusty quality to the air, the flutter of green curtains and the softness of night. This home was all we ever had.

After several minutes, I went to the basement, where I crawled onto my futon and quietly, with my face to my jacket, cried again. Not long after, someone opened the basement door. They walked quickly without switching on the lights, and I knew that it was Tomi.

He sat on the edge of the futon near my feet. He said nothing, and I didn't need him to. It was a sensation I used to get as a child, the feeling of someone you love resting at the foot of your bed, after they've told a story, when there's nothing left to say. I listened to Tomi breathe, small-lunged, stuffy-nosed. He built up air a few times like he wanted to say something but remained quiet. Then I felt his weight gradually leave the futon, but before heading upstairs, Tomi came back and set something beside my face. I squinted through the darkness. A pillow.

"You've had them the whole time?" I asked.

Tomi paused on the stairs. He looked over his shoulder, his glasses catching what little light was between us. "Why?" he asked. "Do you need another one?"

# ANY FURTHER WEST

......................

I grew up in an adobe home with my mother and grandmother in Saguarita, Colorado. It was only us girls. There had never been any men. My mother used to say that her father died at the hands of a madman over a gold watch, but once my grandmother told me the only hands that killed him were his own. As for my father, he took my mother on one date to a drive-in theater on Alonzo Lane. "And you, my baby," my grandmother would say years later, "are the reason nice girls don't sit in cars with boys."

She was a small shadowy woman, my grandmother. She kept an herb garden in the backyard, hung her laundry on metal cords, and occasionally snapped the necks of chickens with an elegant flick of the wrist. Every morning of her life she woke up exhausted. "I'm too damn old to still be raising children," she'd say. "And I don't mean you, Neva." She was talking about my mother, Desiree Leticia Cordova. Throughout her life she had struggled with booze and dope and all those good-for-nothing men. In her twenties, she danced in a strip club on the edge of town called Wishes. In her thirties, the small portion of them she got to live, she uprooted us to California during one of her ecstatic breaks from perpetual sadness. These breaks were infrequent but potent and gave my mother the strength of ten women who require no sleep and live for their whims.

I was twelve when my mother called me into her bedroom one evening before work. She stumbled around in search of a gold bikini, the radio on a doo-wop station, the air reeking of her curling iron. After pulling the bikini from a mound of wrinkled clothes on the floor, she lifted her tank top and applied makeup over her cesarean scar. The red slash eased away, and she peered at herself in the vanity's dust-speckled mirror. "This town is a real dump," she said. "It doesn't offer us enough opportunities. I'm making some big plans. I'm thinking San Diego with all that sunshine."

We left two months later. My mother convinced a white-haired cowboy who worked in oil and gas to give her a couple thousand dollars. She claimed the money meant nothing to him because he had more of it than God. My grandmother told me that was bullshit. "There are chains attached to cash," she said. I pictured mustached men in Stetson hats rattling their linked steel arms. I didn't want to leave home, but I knew if I stayed with my grandmother in Saguarita, my mother would have no one but those chains.

The day we left, I loaded the car as my mother handed me luggage and supplies—cookbooks, rain jackets, batteries, potato chips. Through the haze of early morning, I saw our home anchored to the earth, a short slant above sage grass, seated before the sapphire mountains. As the sun broke completely over the land, my grandmother stepped outside in a quilted apron and pink house shoes. She held a cup of tea, the waves of steam stopping just short of her jaw. She squinted at us. "It's going to rain along the way. You pull off if it pours."

"Of course I know that, Mama," said my mother.

My grandmother glanced at me. "Take care of her, and for Christ's sake, Desiree, take care of yourself."

Eula Court curved like a shark's fin from one green gully filled with trash to another. Rows of rainbow-colored houses flickered by until my mother parked the car outside a boxy home, sunshine yellow with white trim. She checked her reflection in the rearview mirror, blotting her wide forehead and deep cleavage with a napkin. She applied sparkly lip gloss. She adjusted her spaghetti straps.

"This," I said, pointing with my index finger, "is where we're going to live?"

"We're number two," she said. "The place in back, a carriage house."

I followed my mother to the main house, where she rang the doorbell and gently knocked. From behind her, I could make out her shoulder bones, ridged, as if her skeleton had been shattered and glued hastily back together. When the door opened and we were ushered inside by a man's high-pitched voice, my mother's back disappeared, swallowed by indoor dimness. There was only a black leather sofa and a television in the front room. A youngish man in flip-flops and a puka shell necklace stood before us with sloppy brown hair, done in the style girls at my old school called the lazy freshness. He introduced himself as Casey, the landlord.

"Hope the drive was easy for you, ladies," he said, his chin tilted upward. "You're sure going to love this place."

Casey helped us unload the car. He moved with uncoordinated enthusiasm. The carriage house, he explained, was a lot like his house only miniature. After pointing out the gas stove, the water heater, and the vibration we might feel when the garage door beneath us either opened or closed, he patted the pockets on his cargo shorts and produced two sets of keys. "Don't lose them. I'll have to charge you a million bucks."

My mother laughed and swiped his shoulder. "Must have the toughest locks in all of California on these doors."

"Yup. But I keep mine open for the most part."

When he asked if we needed anything else, my mother said everything was fine and thanked him. She watched as he returned to the front house. Between the homes was a small grassy courtyard, his shadowed back windows facing our sunny front ones. "I like him," my mother said after some time. "Seems dependable."


The carriage house was nothing like our home in Saguarita. Palm trees and hibiscus butted against the front door, which opened to a small, elevated stoop where cement steps and a white iron handrail led the way into Casey's courtyard. The stove, the counters, and the tiles were avocado green. My bedroom was a tiny eggshell space, while my mother's was large and airy with her queen-size bed dead center beneath the ceiling fan. Her lacy thrift-store dresses hung in the closet and her plastic jewelry was looped over thumbtacks in the walls. Her perfumes— vanillas and spices, florals and orientals—were displayed atop her vanity. The windows were always open, allowing in stark sunlight and city smells—distant sea salt, car exhaust, In-N-Out burger. "Ah, for the love of God," my grandmother would tell me over the phone. "What a phony paradise."

Soon it was clear my mother needed a job—there was only

enough cash to cover the cost of moving and the first couple months' rent. Because my grandmother wasn't there to stay with me at night, my mother gave up dancing. No matter, she claimed. She was ready for change. Most days before and after school, I'd find her in our kitchen, furiously circling job listings in the paper. She'd stand at the counter, a pen in hand and one leg kicked up behind her like a flamingo. "I think I could do this," she'd say, pointing to an ad for a secret shopper or a dog walker. I saw commercials on TV advertising dental assistant school and massage therapy classes. When I suggested she do something like that, my mother always laughed. "We don't have the money for school, jita. Plus, I'm not one for studying."

Though the prospect of her landing a decent, well-paying job seemed far-fetched, she never let on that we should worry about rent or food. Not even birthday cake.

That November I turned thirteen. "You're my everything, mi vida," my mother said as she pushed a cart through the grocery store. She wore a large shoulder purse and dirty platform sandals. Her black liner was smudged around her eyes, and I worried she had been crying. That morning she gave me a shoe box. Inside was a sheet of white paper on which she had written: *Once I get a job, this will be whatever you want. Love, Mama.* I carried the note in my pocket as the cart rattled and whined throughout the aisles. Sixties pop music played from the ceiling speakers. My mother's hips swayed to the sounds, only pausing when she held up various items—Milano cookies, ice cream bars, tres leches cake.

"Any of these?" she asked.

Beside us a white woman in shiny sandals glared in our direction. I lowered my voice. "We don't have the money, Mama."

"Come on, Neva. Whatever you want. It's your day." She waved a box of Nutter Butters in my face. "These are your favorite."

I shook my head. "But we can't."

My mother kissed my forehead, leaving the waxy feeling of her peach lipstick. I turned away while she threw the cookies into the cart. She went through the aisles, tossing in more items—cupcakes, scented candles, avocados, olives, maraschino cherries. After some time, my mother pushed the cart behind a pyramid of canned soda. She unzipped her purse, and it swallowed everything as though it were a bottomless, hungry mouth. When she was done, the only items in the cart were the Nutter Butters and a jar of mayonnaise. My mother smacked her gum as the clerk rang her up for $7.34. From her bra, she handed over a limp ten-dollar-bill. I looked to the floor at my jelly sandals, at the grime in the grooves of the polished cement, at my mother's pristine blue toenail polish. Then I saw flip-flops. Casey stood behind us with a basket of hummus and eggs.

"Must be a party tonight," he said, eyeing our cookies and mayonnaise.

My mother turned, brightened her eyes with a smile. "It *is* a party. Neva's turning thirteen today. We're going to Balboa Park to celebrate."

"Welcome to your teen years, chica." Casey held his fingers above different chocolates along the register, said he was feeling them for *vibes*. He tossed a packet of M&M's onto the black conveyor belt along with his hummus and eggs. "Happy birthday, kid. Hope you like the kind with peanuts."

"I'm allergic," I lied.

My mother bumped me with her purse. "If you're not busy, why don't you join us?"

On the eastern edge of Balboa Park, the three of us sat on a

Mexican blanket in the grass near a pond of koi fish. My mother set out the stolen food, and if Casey knew we didn't pay, he said nothing. He lay there with his arms folded beneath his neck, his green eyes cloudy and his smile slightly crooked with his chemically whitened teeth. With my mother nestled beside him, he spoke of surfing accidents, killer earthquakes, and all-night beach bonfires. My mother told him she loved the ocean and that as a little girl she'd dreamed of its deep and bright creatures. As the sun lowered in the sky, a warm breeze tugged at the pond's surface and the two of them sang "Happy Birthday" to me. I blew out a stolen candle stuffed into a stolen cupcake and worried the entire time that strangers might mistake us for a family.

Casey didn't work. He could barely fix our drains when they clogged with ropes of black hair. Mostly he collected rent checks from the different properties his parents had given him down by the border and further inland in those neighborhoods I never saw. Each morning he cut through the horror-movie fog of the city, running alongside the shores of the Pacific. When he returned, he would shower and then knock on our door, where he flirted with my mother, leaning against our doorframe, the sky behind him blisteringly white. By mid-October he cut us a deal on rent, and by November there was no rent to pay at all.

Thanksgiving, a time when the mountains of Saguarita were bleached with snowfall, our yard in California was an eruption of fuchsia flowers and mazelike palms. I was relieved that school was out for break. Though I was friendly with a few girls who read *Teen Beat* and *YM* magazines during lunch, I kept mostly to myself. Perhaps that's why my teacher always called me Natalie or Maria—anything but my name. When I told my grandmother about this over the phone, she groaned with irritation. "And has your mama found a job yet?" I didn't tell her that my mother wasn't looking for work anymore. That she wasn't doing much besides spending time with Casey.

It was early December when I walked home from school one Friday afternoon and heard them arguing in the front house. The windows were open and the sounds of classic rock and my mother's cries spilled into the street. *You promised us a deal,* she kept saying. *I'll have to go back to dancing.* A group of boys from my middle school walked home across the block, toward one of the trash-filled gullies. Two boys giggled, patting the others on the shoulders, pointing for them to listen. I tossed my backpack on the sidewalk.

"Hey, morons," I shouted, "mind your own business."

The boys turned to look at me. They blinked, scrunched their faces. One of them mouthed *What the——*. He held up his right hand, displaying an orange Game Boy as bright as a flare. They weren't listening to my mother and Casey; they were trying to beat a high score. With my cheeks burning red, I looped around the block three times before I went home.

When I got back, Casey stepped onto his porch in sunglasses, a beach towel slung over his arm. My mother appeared behind him in the darkness of the house—her arm slithering down his chest. "Do you want to go to Mission Beach with us?" she asked. "There's a roller coaster there." They were both obviously drunk or stoned, maybe both. My mother asked again if I'd go. She walked outside and kneeled down to me. She ran her long fingernails along my neck, sending warmth down my spine. "Please come," she said. "I'll get you a kite. Everyone loves a kite."

At Mission Beach, Casey bought me a funnel cake and gave me quarters to play old-timey arcade games. We went out on the pier and my mother got a kite with a plastic handle. She started it in the wind before handing it to me. It shifted up and dropped before it got caught beneath the pier. I left it dangling in the surf. On the boardwalk, we waited in line for the roller coaster. Casey slipped his hand in my mother's back pocket. She giggled and leaned into him. We rode the roller coaster before the sunset. I sat behind them, marveling at the way they both jerked a little too much and a little too late as the coaster curved.

That Sunday my mother slept until the evening. While she was in bed, I read a mystery paperback on the living room floor. Children were science experiments gone wrong. They had broken wings and X-ray vision. Their parents were mad researchers. I finished the book just before the room faded from dusk to night in several slow minutes. I tried waking up my mother then, first by shaking her and then with something to eat. On the gas stove, I warmed flour tortillas, covered them with butter and sugar, and brought them to her side. She let out a few wet snores, turning herself over and away from me. I ate the tortillas myself before crawling beside her. When she woke up later, I asked what was wrong.

"Everything stays the same," she said. "Nothing changes. It makes me feel like I'm dead."

"You're just sad today, Mama. You'll feel better tomorrow." I hugged her and after a long silence, I said, "Tell me a story?"

"About what, Neva? You know all my stories."

"How about me? What was it like when I was born?"

My mother moaned and adjusted herself. I reached for her hand, weaving her slender fingers, limp as lace, into mine. "It was snowing. I was so tired and Grandma was so tired. They cut you out of me because you wouldn't come for hours." She took our hands, moving them beneath the blankets and sheets, halting at her cesarean scar. "Here. This is where you came from. You cried and cried. The doctors said you cried so much you'd never need to cry again. They were right. You never cry, Neva. You're always tough." She paused a moment, and we both were quiet.

"Now you," she said in a tone of rising hopefulness. "You tell me a story."

I had no idea what to say. All my stories were her stories. I considered the things I knew that I wanted her to know, too. Like how much I hated California, how little I knew or liked Casey. But instead, I told her this: "Did you know the palm trees in our yard and all over this neighborhood, they aren't from San Diego? They aren't even from California. We learned about it in school. They don't belong here. Someone just thought they looked pretty."

"No," my mother said. "I didn't know that." She then stopped talking and fell asleep. I would have stayed there with her forever if not for the knock on our door an hour later when Casey stopped by, inviting us to dinner.

When I told my grandmother about my mother's new boyfriend and her staying in bed until nighttime, she wanted us home immediately. She called my mother every day to talk sense into her. It wasn't good for me, she claimed. I needed structure and family. She said my mother should attend Mass regularly, visit confession. When my mother stopped taking her calls, my grandmother sent letters addressed to Desiree Leticia in elegant, shaky script. Though she didn't have the money for a flight and she was too old to drive any further west, my grandmother made sure we felt her presence. In one of her letters, she begged my mother to remember her father. "He let the world beat him down, break him," she wrote. "He allowed the world to fill up on his sadness."

A week before Christmas, Casey and my mother ate sunflower seeds and passed a bottle of whiskey between them on the beach. They took long swallows, wilting into one another, sloppy and euphoric. We were near the pier, the underside of its wooden belly bleached. Surfers in bodysuits ran beneath the stilts, their boards in hand. Faded blue tattoos winked across the backs of old men with salty hair. The ocean's howl was wild.

"Neva," Casey said. "It means snow, right? In Latin or something?"

I shrugged, slipping my hand beneath the cool sand.

"Sure does," said my mother. "Her grandma picked it out. It was blizzarding when Neva was born. If we lived here, maybe we would've named her Sunshine or Sunny." My mother giggled, a seed flying from her mouth.

"I like it," Casey said. "It's different. You like the beach, Neva?"

I told him the beach was all right.

"That's not true," my mother blurted out. "You love the beach." She turned to Casey. "The first time we came here I couldn't pry her away from the water. She kept splashing and screaming when the waves hit her little toes."

Casey laughed. "How about for Christmas Eve we drive up the coast? There's a beachfront motel in Solana. A buddy of mine can get us a deal on a boat. I figure since you have no family here and my folks are in Florida we could go together."

My mother fell into him, landing a kiss mostly on his mouth. "Sounds perfect, baby."

Casey nudged me with his shoulder. "Come on, chica. It's my treat."

I rose from our beach blanket and headed toward the water. "Be careful," I heard my mother shout. "It'll be freezing."

There was no line between ocean and sky. White gulls appeared black in the clouds' shadows. I unzipped my jacket and rolled my jeans to my knees. Though the sand was uneven and fine and the water dim, I walked ahead until my legs were soaked. It only burned a moment before my skin went numb. In school we learned the entire southwest desert was once underwater. Everywhere was a shallow sea. My mother sometimes told me she felt like she was drowning. She had dreams of waking up dead, dreams of sleeping forever. But what about me? I asked more than once, and she always said I was lucky. Lucky because I knew how to swim. As I moved through the waves, my mother and Casey were still on the shore, their legs entangled like four pale links in the same gate. One of the surfers bobbed past me, shouting for me to head back.

At the beach blanket, I stood above my mother and Casey. The sun had come out, my shadow long over their faces. "You were right, Mama," I said. "It's freezing out there."

"It will be a great Christmas," my mother said as she packed four bags for our one-night stay in Solana Beach. "Probably the best Christmas we've ever had." She stood at her closet, selecting summer dresses for the dead of winter. Wedge heels, corked sandals, and floppy sunhats. I lay across her bedspread, wondering at the way her back disappeared into darkness as she pushed forward into her clothes. She turned around with an armful of bathing suits. She asked me to choose one. I pointed to a bikini with red polka dots. My mother changed before me, sliding her panties down her legs beneath her T-shirt. She pulled on the suit bottoms, secured the top's strings, and sheepishly turned to face me, her left arm over her stomach.

"This one?" she asked. "It doesn't make me look fat?"

"Of course not, Mama."

Though her figure was tight and trim, a holdover from her years as a dancer, in nature there were no forgiving club lights. There was only the sun and its unrelenting shine. My mother reminded me of this as she twirled, all black hair and swinging arms. "What about my scar?"

"I've seen it a thousand times."

"But Casey hasn't. I never let him see it in the light."

"Who cares?" I suggested.

My mother had me pick another bathing suit. In the end, she went with a one-piece, all white with scooped-out hips. She then disappeared once more into her closet. She reemerged with a small wooden box. She set it before me, urging me to open it. I unlatched the brass clasp delicately, but my mother laughed, taking my hands in hers. "No need to be gentle, baby. It's not the box that's special." Inside was a charm bracelet with only three charms. A baby rattle, a chicken, a locket. My mother spun the bracelet around my wrist, stopping at the locket.

"When you were two, you came down with this bad fever," she said. "You were so hot that I could barely touch you." My mother opened the locket, revealing two tufts of dark hair. "Grandma said you'd die if we didn't bring it down. I gave you cold baths. You didn't cry at all. You just sat in the tub shivering. I prayed all night and in the morning, just like that, you were better. Calm and smiling and the right temperature. So you know what I did?"

"No," I said, "I can't remember."

My mother kissed my head. "I cut off a piece of your hair. Fever hair, I called it. I put it in this locket with a piece of my own hair. I don't know why, but it makes me happy to have us together like that."

I felt the weight of the bracelet on my wrist. I thought of how strange it would be to touch someone so hot with fever you could barely hold them. I had never felt someone like that, and I wondered if I ever would.

That night, TV static like snow played in my mind as I moved between sleeplessness and dreams. I imagined laughter, the kind you hear walking alongside playgrounds with small children making use of every object, a stick to the fence, a foot to the ear, their telephone call home. I saw lush flowers, lemon and orange trees, and volcanic rock gardens that were beautiful instead of strange to me at Christmastime. I pictured Casey driving us to Solana Beach, whizzing past lurching shorelines and multimillion-dollar glass houses. I felt the salty mist of La Jolla's cliffs and heard the enormous barking seals. I thought of my mother. I thought of napping beside her in a large motel bed beneath windows open to the sea.

But Casey didn't come for us, and while I wasn't surprised, my mother went through stages of disbelief. She sat very still in our kitchen, drinking what little vodka she found in the freezer. *Maybe he was sick? Maybe there was an accident? Maybe he needed help?* She smoked a pack of Marlboro Lights without bothering to open the windows. A single line emerged between her eyebrows, difficult to read beneath the resting smoke. When she eventually realized he wasn't coming, she called him every name in the book, chaining together the insults like an endless train of *cocksucker*s and *motherfucker*s and *asshole*s. "He's a bad guy," she said firmly with her final cigarette between two fingers, resting against her temple. "Just another piece of shit."

I tried to stop her as she barreled down the cement steps, heading toward the front house. She was going to destroy something, herself or otherwise. I watched in awe as she slipped into rage as easily as she had slipped into her bathing suit. She pounded with her fists on his windows and tossed rocks at his mailbox. She threw mud across his door. When she finished, her fingernails broken and lined with dirt, there wasn't much to do but sit on the stoop and watch as one by one Christmas lights flickered along our block. After some time, my mother began to cry, quietly at first until she heaved uncontrollably, her back to me, her shoulder blades quivering in their jagged way. I kneeled down to her, holding her face to mine with both hands. We were matted together in her tears.

"Will you nap with me, baby?" she asked.

I told her yes. I pulled her from the stoop.

She lay beside me in bed. It was warm, though the windows were open and the ceiling fan was on high. I pushed the bedspread onto the floor when my mother's back grew sticky with sweat. Her eyelids squeezed, her lashes fluttered. "I think we're done here, Neva. I think it's best we go home."

At four in the morning, a deep vibration shook the bed. It was the garage door opening. Casey was back. My mother woke up, making a sound like she was catching her breath. She ran to him in the courtyard. I watched them argue through the front windows. Something about a flat tire, a friend's flat tire, difficult properties down on the border. My mother's hair flew around her face, covering her eyes. Her nightgown was transparent and she was naked beneath the thin fabric. As she spoke to Casey, my mother covered her belly, hiding her midsection's

scar. That's when I went back to bed and listened to their fighting until my mother came inside just before sunrise. She grabbed
face wash from our bathroom and stood in my doorframe. We
looked at one another.

"Don't worry," she said, breathless. "I'm not upset anymore."

She turned and stepped into the hallway, locking the door of
the carriage house before she left for Casey's.


On Christmas morning, I woke up from a dream of snow. When
we lived in Saguarita, I would have run to the living room to
hug my mother, kiss my grandmother, and open my stocking
filled with practical gifts. The kind no one wants but everyone
needs—socks, underwear, floss, ChapStick. I walked through
my mother's bedroom and opened her closet. My face was
against her things. Cheek to sleeve, lips to collar, nose to cotton.
I fell into her jackets and blouses, dresses and skirts. I breathed
in, smelling a thousand different spices, all of them sweet.

Outside the fog had rolled in, low to the earth, seeping into
the asphalt and grass. I found my mother loading the car,
hunched down in a long white dress and straw hat, two braids
falling around her shoulders. She waved to me as I stepped
barefoot over the cement path from Casey's house to the street.
The sky was all clouds with a single prominent streak, an airplane's tail sailing east. My mother slammed the trunk before
turning to me on the sidewalk. Her eyes were large black pools.
Her face was dewy and young, just as it was the day we arrived
in California. "Hurry now," she said. "Grab your bags."

"Where are we going?" I asked. "Home?"

My mother clicked her tongue, stifling a laugh. "We're going
to the beach with Casey. Remember?" I looked at her face for a

long while hoping to catch a hint of sarcasm, an eyebrow raised, an upper lip curled. But my mother only smiled with faintly blue lips, moving her fingers through the air, edging me on with beautiful wide nails. Behind me Casey walked outside in sunglasses, briefly lifting them from his face as he pulled my mother in for a kiss. With closed eyes they knocked against the car door. My mother's hat flew from her head, exposing her wide forehead before swirling into the sky and landing swiftly at my toes. I picked up the hat, bringing it to my mother, who took it gently from my hands, the noble arcs of her thumbs mirroring my own. The air went still between us as I grazed her skin, so cool and strange, nearly dead.

Casey asked, "You don't feel well, chica?"

I told him I was fine.

"Then hurry," said my mother.

Her stance was wobbly and unrefined, as though she had given someone else permission to wear her skin. That's when I knew she was forever caught in her own undercurrent, bouncing from one deep swell to the next. She would never lift me out of that sea. She would never pause to fill her lungs with air. Soon the world would yank her chain of sadness against every shore, every rock, every glass-filled beach, leaving nothing but the broken hull of a drowned woman. I turned away from my mother then, heading toward the carriage house, whispering *no* so many times that I sounded like a cooing dove. My mother asked more than once for me to stop. The further I walked, the further her voice moved from giddy to shrill, rising above the hibiscus and palm trees, booming off the front house and carriage house doors.

# ALL HER NAMES

. . . . . . . . . . . . . . . . .

Michael was aging. His smile was young but the slack of his skin and the hollows of his face belonged to someone much older than thirty-three. He was a sales manager at a medium-size marijuana dispensary on Colfax Avenue that resembled a cellphone store, complete with kiosks of edibles and cases of "hardware." Whenever Alicia's husband, Gary, left town for his annual auctioneers' convention, she called Michael. She recognized her inability to spend an evening alone. That, and she still loved Michael. Probably always would.

When night fell, Alicia slipped into his old teal Nova, a vision out of a lowrider magazine, even if the interior was a pigsty. She could see a crumpled sweatshirt, some woman's black tights, and three empty spray-paint cans on the floor. Alicia picked up one of the cans. It rattled like pebbles as she rolled it across Michael's lap. "Keep this shit in the trunk. Joaquin got charged with a felony last summer."

"Only because that pendejo couldn't outrun the bull. Besides, someone has to make these invasive yuppies uncomfortable. Weedy motherfuckers. Growing out of control." In his worn leather jacket, Michael gestured toward Gary and Alicia's concrete-and-glass house, a black square among the updated Victorians. "Where to, my little gentrification Malinche?"

"Lawrence Street."

"Why the hell we going there, Cia?"

"It's my dogs. Fleas. All over their ankles and behind their ears."

"Have you considered the vet?"

"No, no," said Alicia. "They need that real medicine, that herbal stuff."


Their names were Kane and Oscar, Gary's from before the marriage, black Labs always in hysterics. Alicia tolerated the dogs, only shuddered at their clumsy galloping, their narrow bodies twisting around the end tables and chairs. That morning, after wrangling them into the backyard, where Kane, her least liked, gnawed an entire fallen tree branch, Alicia went upstairs to discover that she was pregnant for the second time in her life. She was twenty-nine, thirty in a week, a perfectly acceptable age to have a child, but Alicia felt dread. Almost grief. She was wrapped in a white bath towel, hunched over the toilet, as she broke the plastic pregnancy test in two, burying it beneath the unused tampons and wadded Kleenex. She wouldn't tell a soul, not even Gary. Especially not Gary, who'd had so much to say lately about her biological clock.

They'd been married two years. Gary was fifty-four, a spry white-haired auctioneer from Nebraska who owned the largest farm and automotive equipment auction yard in Denver. He'd been interested in reaching a wider, Spanish-speaking audience

when he first saw Alicia at a meeting for the Univision net-
work. "You," he told the twenty-six-year-old graphic designer,
"have a great fuckin' nose." Alicia grew to call him her rancher,
her vaquero, her daddy. Gary simply called her by a childhood
nickname—Ali Bird. She liked him to call out, with his auctioneer's tongue, this name in bed. All her names, really. Alicia
Monica del Toro, and, later, Alicia Monica del Toro Parker.

Not long after the wedding, Gary took Alicia on a weekend
trip to Key West, where they chartered a speedboat called *Con-
tender* and rode out to meet the sunset across the glassy plane.
With the sea breeze strangely still and their faces warmed by
rum, Gary held his wife from behind. "We'd make some damn
good-looking kids," he said.

"You already have two dogs. What more do you need?"

"Give me just one, Ali Bird. A son to carry on my name."

"You don't need a son for that," she said. "I carry that
name."

Botánica del Cobre sat adjacent to Tacos Jalisco, a narrow food
counter with a limited selection of carnitas and tequila. Michael
insisted on stopping there before anywhere else. "Just a shot or
two, you know, to get the night rolling." It was packed with a
few Mexicano families, several Chicano rockabilly couples, and
of course, a smattering of Anglo newcomers, white kids in Carhartt hoodies and Red Wing shoes, the clothing of work they'd
never know. "I hate 'em," Michael said, clearing salt from his
bottom lip. A young bleached blonde in a crop top eyed him
from the soda fountain, obvious and driven. "I'll screw 'em, but
I hate 'em."

"Story of your life." Alicia wasn't as irritated as Michael by
the influx of Denver residents. Mostly, she imagined, because

she lived among them, greeted them by name at the dog park, walked alongside their designer strollers on Saturday mornings.

"You can handle it, Cia." Michael scooted a glass of Hornitos across the table.

"Watching my figure." Alicia wasn't sure she believed this, but it sounded plausible. "Come on, del Cobre's closing soon."

Michael tossed back the second shot. Beneath the table, he cupped Alicia's knee, a muscle memory pat. "That's one place," he said, "that I'd be happy to see close for good." He smiled at Alicia. "For the record."

It had been over a decade, she thought, since they first visited the botánica. Alicia's father was dying of liver cancer brought on by years of working the uranium mines outside Denver. The doctors prescribed morphine, OxyContin, fentanyl patches. Nothing masked his agony without shutting down his brain. "That's it," Alicia's abuela Lopez told her one autumn afternoon. "Your papa deserves to die with dignity of mind." She sent Alicia and Michael down Lawrence Street with a piece of paper on which she had written a list of herbs in her shaky script. When they returned to his bedside, Alicia's father held her hand and asked in an empty voice, "Were you in the garden, Stephanie?" That was the worst part, how toward the end he often confused Alicia with her mother, Stephanie Elkhorn, an Anglo woman who, when Alicia was four, packed her purses and thrift-store dresses and didn't come back.

They entered the botánica to the ringing of bells, a banana rind tied around the brass doorknob. Protection or warning. Either way, some kind of brujería. The walls were covered in crucifixes and mirrors, rodent skulls, and santo candles. An old man wearing several orange and black necklaces lounged in a lawn chair, catching the end of some sports program on a decades-old radio. He fiddled with the antenna and waved at Michael and Alicia, motioning toward a bilingual sign on the counter: *Ask me about free cleansings for New Yr. Bring eight lilies & 1 coconut. Must wear white.*

Michael pulled Alicia near, speaking warmly through her hair. "For the dogs, right?"

She shushed him, pressing him away with an open palm. "Excuse me," she said to the clerk.

A woman in a pink frock, her back slightly curved, emerged from behind a beaded curtain. She stepped onto a wooden box, standing tall at the long counter with display cases of fresh cow hearts and dried cobra skins. "¿Les puedo ayudar en algo?"

Alicia only spoke enough Spanish to bump her way through a sales transaction. When she was growing up, Abuela Lopez sometimes spoke to her in a southern Colorado dialect, almost archaic. Michael's family was from Bakersfield, making him useless unless you needed Spanish slang for *pussy* and *40 ounce*. Alicia checked that he was out of earshot when she asked, in her broken Spanish, for an herb called neem.

"¿Para?"

Alicia flashed the canary diamond on her left hand, out of shame or conceit, she couldn't decide which. She then turned her back to Michael, pointing to her womb.

"No se garantiza que funcione; y también duele."

Alicia nodded.

"Entonces ya lo sabe," said the clerk. "Lo sabe mejor que yo."

"No way," Michael hollered from across the botánica, "this incense is made from, I shit you not, viper sperm. What the heck?"

Alicia ignored him as the woman headed into the back room.

. . . . . . .

The sounds of the radio cracked away from sports and into conjunto music. When the clerk reappeared, she held what looked like an urn and gave explicit directions to steep the leaves in boiling water for half an hour. Alicia said gracias, paying in cash.

Outside the moon was nearly full.

"Fleas?" Michael asked as they walked toward the Nova, their shadows slim on the grainy, amber-colored asphalt. He opened the passenger door with his key. "I don't like it when you lie, Cia."

She faced him, studied an L-shaped wrinkle across his cheek. "I'm pregnant. I don't want it. The end."

"You should tell Gary, if you haven't. It's the right thing to do."

Alicia turned away from Michael as he shut her inside the car. It was colder than before, the light shining in such a way that the moment seemed slow, as if time had slightly realigned to another beat. "It's not really any of his business," she said. "And it's none of yours, either."


They parked the Nova outside an abandoned adult theater on Twenty-third Street. The lot sloped into a cement trail that ran along the South Platte River, leading to the Union Pacific rail yard and Confluence Park, a spot where, over 150 years earlier, according to Alicia's freshman history class at UCD, Denver was founded when an Anglo named William Greeneberry Russell discovered gold and the city erupted. Before that, it was an Arapahoe camp. Now it was a desolate hillside filled with stoners and the homeless, flanked by multimillion-dollar condos and public art. The new Queen City of the Plains.

They moved toward the river, a row of Section 8 apartments

on the left. Alicia remembered her first place after Abuela Lopez died and the bank took the house on Galapago Street. It was a basement studio with subterranean windows and cruel lighting. Cobwebs and spider sacs appeared often. Alicia would open the window, shoot a stream of ammonia from a spray bottle, and break the sacs against the corrugated steel lining the glass. They never had problems with insects on Galapago, though once while riding her bike past the old house, Alicia saw an Anglo woman in a purple dress gingerly directing a group of exterminators through the yard. *Watch your step,* she had said. *The new owners are still improving the foundation.*

Michael and Alicia halted before a human-size cut in a chain-link fence. The whole of the Union Pacific rail yard was visible, an elegant expanse of routes sending trains north into Wyoming, east into Kansas, and west, through mountain passes and white-out valleys, into Utah, a journey ending in California sunlight. Alicia loved the idea of her name riding so far. Not Alicia del Toro Parker, but her tag name—K-SD, easily pronounced *cased.* Michael reached for Alicia's hand, but she smacked him away. She climbed through, effortlessly. He followed, the fence trembling.

At the yard's western edge, they searched out a clean freight. Within the aisles of tracks, Michael and Alicia passed the ghost-like shapes of hoppers and field mice stalked by feral cats. The bodies of homeless men sunk into the jagged banks of the yard, their busted boots and clumped sleeping bags gray mounds among the dirt. Michael lit a cigarette. Beneath the yard lights, his face seemed younger, his teeth ivory, his eyes shining. They continued on past empty cars with crude tags by amateurs. There were massive DEKO signatures, left by a long-standing Denver crew with gangbanger tendencies. Michael exhaled his smoke, pointing to a character tag, SNOOPY with chicken scratch beneath it: MILE HI CITY. He hated this shit, and she agreed. They moved behind a yellow switcher where, some twenty yards ahead, was a water tower with a silhouette of a K-SD piece. Michael said, "All I remember was climbing that rickety ladder"—he paused, adding, as if for good measure—"your ass in front of me the whole way."

"Good God. Let's hit this train, already."

With their backpacks heavy, they rushed the tracks, the iron walls forming a canyon in the night. It was like old times, when they were young and Michael was enough. Alicia bumped him with her right shoulder. "I always think of you, Mikey. When a train rolls by my place at one A.M., it's all you." She loved the trains, how they charged forward, creating their own sense of time.

"Me, too," he said. "I hear the sounds of the tracks rattling, the horns blaring, and those caution gates getting lowered. It gets me all hot. Then I turn to the chick beside me in bed and say, 'This reminds me of my ex-girlfriend.'"

Alicia stopped walking, her boots hitting the ground with a smack. "You're an asshole. I don't want to hear that."

"Why not, Cia? You're the married one. Same dish every night."

"I don't see why you have to jab, that's all." In the far distance, she spotted their freight, clean under shadows, a track pointed toward Kansas.

"You don't know why?" Michael said.

The first time, it was Michael's. Alicia was nineteen. At the King Soopers on Speer Boulevard, she shoved an E.P.T box into her unseasonably warm coat and biked to the house she shared with her abuela Lopez. Alicia took the test in her upstairs bath-

. . . . . . . .

room, later emptying the wastebasket in a nearby park. A clinic doctor prescribed a pill that knifed Alicia's insides for three days and two nights. On the third day, dizzy and partially blind with pain, Alicia staggered into the kitchen, where she found Abuela Lopez standing at the counter chopping pork with a butcher's knife. It was spring. The windows were open. The perfume of lilacs pushed into the house and mixed with the stench of raw meat.

"Abuelita," she said, "I need to tell you something." Before Alicia could finish, Abuela Lopez missed the pork, slicing her right thumb, blood flowing over the meat.

Abuela Lopez called her granddaughter many names that day. Selfish, cruel, stupid, childish. When she got the bleeding under control and her temper sealed away, she told Alicia, "Before all this bullshit, we only had the herbs, mija. Why didn't you ask me?" Abuela Lopez knew what plants to use, the temperature at which to sip the tea, how many cups for how many days, how long the cramps would curl Alicia's insides, and to what extent she should expect tenderness in her breasts.

They agreed on the freight. Michael walked to one side while Alicia went to the other. She removed her gloves and ran her hands over the chilled steel. Weeks before, Alicia had planned her design, a navy signature centered with slim text, white gradient shading, a black circle in her K. Michael always told her that he didn't like K-SD much, that Alicia should write something else, something clearly feminine. But Michael's wasn't much better. SLOKE. Who would write that? And what the hell did it mean? They pulled the cans of Rust-Oleum from their bags and began painting. It was odd how it worked. Alicia did countless designs for work, but when it came to trains, some unknowable engine drove her hands. On more than one occasion, in more than one dirt lot, Alicia experienced the feeling of seeing her signature appear, as if she had uncovered it beneath the dirty metal.

With her scarf covering her nose and mouth, Alicia rested in the midst of her long dash, peeking around the car's edge at Michael, who never looked better than when he was writing. He worked his spray can gracefully, his dark eyes focused only on SLOKE. In the triangular space between his outstretched arm and neck, a far-off streetlamp formed a spiral of light. "How's it going?"

"Half finished. You still on your second letter?"

"My dash. The edges are so clean, so nice. You wouldn't know about it."

Michael shook his can, started again. "Oh, Cia, I know about that dash."

"You're an idiot."

"I know," Michael said with pride.

A low vibration rattled the track. A ghost train rolling. An engine firing. Michael and Alicia stiffened as they examined the rails. They once knew a kid who died in the yards. He wasn't much older than sixteen. It was the middle of summer, early at night. The bull hadn't come out to patrol. The kid was painting a train when he took a step back and a single freight rolled over him. Word spread among crews, and soon kids visited the unfinished signature, painting their wishes in black. A poem appeared. *May your journey be an endless track / may your trains keep rolling / may your name be completed when you're back.*

Alicia kicked the freight, a booming sound. "Someone's been practicing."

"Get to work, Cia. Who knows the next time you'll get—"

Light flashed over his face, not the floodlights or the streetlamps, but a concentrated stream. Michael squinted as Alicia tried to dodge the white rays, spinning around to search the rails.

Cops. Some twenty yards behind.

Tossing their backpacks beneath the car, they set off, Michael in the lead, cutting corners, jumping tracks. They had run before, and they knew the course. At the border of the yard and Confluence Park, Alicia climbed a chain-link fence, otherworldly, lithe, as though she'd lift into the sky and join the stars. But she only fell back to earth, a quick slap on dead grass. They ran on, keeping pace as two male voices hollered for them to do something like give up, to lay over, to end it. Alicia imagined hounds were tracking them. She stuck out her leg, tripping Michael. Before he could utter a word, she was on top of him, removing her scarf and unzipping her jacket. She pulled her sweater above her breasts and unhooked her bra.

"Just shut up," she whispered. "Don't say shit."

She cupped Michael's hands in hers, guiding them along her stomach, shivering at the chilled smoothness of his palms. She let go, feeling his hands gliding lower to her center. She arched her body upward, her back bending in a kind of release. The flashlight's beam reappeared as two policemen stood at the top of a hillside, witnessing Alicia with the sides of her puffy coat flung open like a gutted animal. Michael lay silent, pinned between her legs. Alicia breathed, waited. The policemen arrived.

"What're you doing?" they said. "Cover yourself."

Alicia snapped around and began to cry. They were no older than twenty, young men with unremarkable faces, one white and blond, the other brown and short, maybe a boy with a name like Mendoza, perhaps a cousin of a cousin. When the blond officer ordered the couple to stand, Alicia rolled onto her feet, inspecting her hands for paint. She then flashed her left hand, a rock sparkling more than any badge. "I'm so embarrassed," she said as Michael stood beside her. "We were on a night walk, celebrating. We're having our first baby."

The same officer asked Michael if this was true.

"Yes, sir. Proud papa got carried away."

"Carried away?" the shorter one asked now. He looked at Alicia's boots, a thin spot of navy paint across the right tip. She moved that leg behind the other. "Did you see anyone come by?"

"No," they both uttered at once.

"But then, again," Michael said, "we weren't really looking."

The officers asked for IDs, though didn't seem surprised when neither Michael nor Alicia could produce one. "Look," the blond said, "congratulations on your baby. I got two myself, little girls. But that doesn't mean you can publicly do whatever you were doing."

"Of course," said Alicia. "I was just so, I don't know, moved."

"We get it," said the shorter one. "You were carried away, moved. What's your name, ma'am?"

"Stephanie. I'm Stephanie Elkhorn. And this is my husband, Gary." Alicia wouldn't look at Michael even as she felt him glaring at her.

"This is a warning, your one and only. Get your things and get out of here." With that, the policemen turned around and marched up the hill, the metal on their boots and hats flickering with moonlight.

Michael and Alicia stood quietly, the city's skyline enclosing them like a lid. They walked the long way back to the Nova, and after several blocks, Michael turned to Alicia. He touched her face, kissed her cheek. He thanked her for saving them. Alicia imagined him like those sea creatures she'd heard about but would never see. They were so far down, in complete darkness, translucent, their guts exposed like broken clocks. "It wouldn't just be more of you," he said. "It'd be more of Gary. More of you both." Michael then zipped Alicia's coat and reached for her scarf, lightly threading it behind her neck. "Alicia del Toro Parker, I can't see you anymore."

For her thirtieth birthday, Gary took Alicia to the cabin on the acres he owned in southern Colorado, near where her family was from in the San Luis Valley, where she'd spent her summers as a kid, where her father was buried. The cabin sat high in the valley, overlooking the sculpted mounds of desert earth. The weather had picked up. An autumn weekend that felt like late spring. Low-slung clouds crept above, their shape-shifting shadows trailing over the white peaks of the Sangre de Cristo Mountains. The land was aflame.

It was late. They drank gin and tonics outside near a large fire. Alicia had come off her weeklong break from drinking, and the booze ran swiftly through her veins. Gary reclined in a wicker chair. Alicia sat across from him. Gazing into the sky, she stood then and stepped away from the fire. She held her drink with one hand and, with the other, pointed to the stars. Kane, behind her, licked the backs of her knees. Alicia hardened her stance, placing her free hand on the dog's collar. She thought of the goddess Diana; she thought of the moon.

"What're you looking at, Ali Bird?" Gary said.

"I've always been able to find the North Star. It was one of those things my dad taught me, so that I'd never get lost. What does it mean that I can't find it tonight?"

"It means you're drunk, birthday girl." Gary laughed, signaling high above them.

The sky was hazed with the dust of a billion stars, a black void that seemed designed yet eternal. Like a small sun, the fire's heat pressed into Alicia, warming her face and arms. She took off her sweater, dropping it to the ground. In the distance, above the dirt road into town, headlights curved along a mountainside, traveling into the dark. There were the sounds of the crackling fire, Alicia's heavy heartbeat, Kane's breathing loudly beside her. The wind shifted as a rush of embers jumped from the flames. Alicia kneeled down to her dog, shielding her watery eyes from smoke. "There it is," she lied. "I can see it now."

# GHOST SICKNESS

· · · · · · · · · · · · · · · ·

Ana sits in a long classroom with many windows and a dated green chalkboard. The room is half empty. It's summer, and enrollment is low for history sections at the university. Lecturer Samantha Brown stands beneath the clock's black hands. She's young with a Ph.D. from an East Coast school Ana has never heard of.

"An interesting anecdote about Leadville," says Brown, "is the tale of two brothers, one living, one dead. In 1875, while digging the dead brother's grave, the living brother struck a silver vein. He immediately left his dead brother's body to freeze in a snowbank, and claimed the mine."

To prepare for the final, Brown is reviewing the entirety of the course. From Lewis and Clark to fur traders and national parks. She's now on silver booms. Ana's notebook is crammed with notes, her blue-ink handwriting sloppier with each passing minute. She is in her usual seat, in the back, near the windows.

"What this story demonstrates is the absolute depravity of

· · · · · · · ·

the West." Brown writes the word *depravity* on the green chalk-board. She circles it. "Think about that."

A student seated in the front row named Colleen raises her hand. "I mean, isn't that illegal?"

Brown graciously answers Colleen's question with a comment on lawlessness. Ana sifts through her backpack, discreetly pulling her cellphone onto her lap, checking for a message from Clifton. Nothing. Only a text from Mom. *Haven't heard from C. Had a job for him. Dinner tonight?* Ana responds. She shifts in her seat and glances outside.

The normally green city is brown with drought. An eye-shadow-blue sky. A dusty-film negative of trees. Ana hopes it rains soon, but more than anything, she hopes that her boy-friend, wherever he is, comes home. Last Thursday, Clifton said he was visiting his grandparents near Shiprock in New Mexico, a windy flatland marked by winged rocks and cloud-like sheep. There's no cell service in their corner of the reservation, a convenient excuse because Clifton often disappears. He has a problem with weariness, a tendency to binge. But that's Clifton, slippery, like a fish.

Mom pushes past Ana with an armful of paper grocery sacks. She stands on her daughter's stone stoop in her maroon scrubs with uneven sweat marks beneath the arms. She is heavy, solid. Despite her heft, or possibly because of it, her face is beautiful with sharp lines along her jaw and cheeks. She has brought Ana three bags of frozen tortillas, a rinsed-out lard bucket of beef stew, and six bananas. Ana hugs Mom with more force than usual.

Mom says, "I'm sick of you so skinny. Don't you ever eat?"

"Yeah, lots of Student Union frozen burritos."

. . . . . . .

"Where's Clifton, anyway?"

"He's picking up extra shifts at the restaurant," Ana lies, lifting a sack of groceries.

"I had a couple jobs for him around the house, sod to move, bathroom needs painting."

Mom invents these tasks for Clifton, a way to look after Ana. She wasn't happy when two years earlier Ana and Clifton moved in together. *A girl shouldn't shack up,* she had said. *You'll age quickly.* But Mom once cared for Clifton more than Ana did. At eleven, he moved next door with his uncle Virgil after his parents were killed on the reservation in a drunken brawl over seventeen dollars. Mom felt sorry for him then. He often followed her around as she did housework. *Tell me another story,* Clifton would ask Mom as she Windexed and swept. *Now, when I was a little girl, my tía brought me to an arroyo in Montrose, where everyone knew the lake monster lived.* Ana, always sick of these dingy tales, didn't stick around to listen.

The women make dinner in the dry warmth of the apartment, a one-bedroom brick box from the late fifties with no air-conditioning. Heat drifts upward from the oak floors. Mom shares the latest gossip. Would you believe it? Grocery shopping for this very meal, she left her cart in line and walked off in search of batteries. When she returned, an Anglo woman accused her of cutting in line. "Oh, it had to be less than a minute, and I had already been there forever. So, this woman tells me, 'I didn't see you at all!' Can you believe that?" Mom shakes her head while chopping onions. She changes the subject, looking hard at her daughter. "How's school, mija?"

"Fine," says Ana, carrying glasses of sun tea to the wobbly table.

"Are you worried about a class?"

"Just History. None of the dates stick. Everything blurs."

"You better get yourself some flash cards." Mom laughs, salting her frying pork. "You can't fail another class."

Ana knows this. If she fails, she'll lose her scholarship, the Displaced Fund, given to the grandchildren of Denver residents, mostly Hispano, who once occupied the Westside neighborhood before it was plowed to make way for an urban campus. Then she'll lose her work-study job at the library. After that, Ana will be back home with Mom. "I'm trying," she says, "hard."

"What kind of history class, anyway?"

"History of the American West."

Mom smiles with gapped teeth. "How the hell you gonna fail that?"

Ana laughs. "You know history was never my favorite subject."

Later that night, when she's alone in the apartment, Ana's cellphone rings with a blocked number. She answers, drowsy with bad dreams. There's only the electric chirp of static between satellites. It must be Clifton, no one else.

"I know it's you," Ana says, propping her body upright against pillows, the room's darkness a blanket of fog. If she could just force him to speak, pull his voice through the phone. When they were kids, Clifton hid for hours in cupboards, beneath stairwells, inside coat closets, anywhere he could disappear. Little hands sticking out from little cracks in doors. *Mom wants us to come down for lunch*, Ana would say. *This isn't funny anymore.*

Ana says into the phone, "Rent's due Thursday."

The amber glow of a streetlamp shines into their bedroom, working its way through the venetian blinds. Bars of light drop in rows, some of it resting against Clifton's tilted dresser drawers, some of it worming along Ana's face and long black hair. She imagines it's Clifton's breath, warm and sticky, in her ear. "Come home, baby. Please."

At the William H. Moffat Library, Ana clocks in at eleven thirty, checking with her supervisor about the day's tasks, and then ventures into the stacks with a cart of periodicals and children's books. She has prepared a study sheet, occasionally glancing at it between cartloads of books. *Otter Mears, Railroad entrepreneur, 1840–1931. Baby Doe Tabor, found dead in a Leadville cabin, ordered diamond pajamas for her toddler. Chief Ouray signed dubious treaties with Whites.*

Ana closes her eyes, tests herself, forgets. After an hour of shelving, she takes a ten-minute break, walking alongside the Museum of Houses at the center of campus, tiny but elegant Victorians once occupied by families with names like Garcia, Santos, Rios. Ana remembers stories from her grandparents—how the block was alive with sounds of screeching children, running sleek in leather booties, their marbles blasting across sandstone sidewalks. *Come wash up,* their young mothers would say, waving aprons like cotton flares. *Your papas will be home soon.*

When Ana returns to the library, she spots Colleen and another girl from history class studying on the second floor near the magazines. They are both blond with sharp features and lengthy, ivory necks. Ana often wonders about students like Colleen—Denver newcomers with trust funds and loft apartments. They came with the tech jobs and legalization of weed, the Great Green Rush, Ana thinks. Clifton says they aren't too bad. They have nice apartments with new paint, all their cars run, and they rarely speak to you in public, two worlds in one space. The longer they stay, however, the more Ana worries that their world is collapsing her own. She tries avoiding the girls and slips behind a stack of government publications.

"Hannah, right?" Colleen stands behind Ana, goofy with chapped lips.

Ana corrects her, placing a golf magazine on the rack.

"Ready for the final?"

"As much as I can be."

"Tina and I actually wanted to ask you a question." Colleen points behind her, the other girl's light eyes dropped to a cell-phone screen. "You always wear such neat turquoise jewelry. Are you from Colorado, like a Native American?"

"I don't know, really. It's complicated. What about you?"

"I'm from Vermont," says Colleen. "Ever been?"

Ana shakes her head. "Maple syrup? Snow?"

Colleen smiles with gummy teeth. She nods enthusiastically. "Mountains, too. Little ones, though."

"Whenever I picture those faraway states," says Ana, returning to her shelving, "I think of white people and dead witches." Ana laughs and watches as Colleen's eyes narrow in confusion. "Kidding."

After work the apartment windows are open, a warm dusk breeze scattering papers like white doves. Ana leans in the doorway, examining the mess. From inside the bedroom, the radio sounds. *It'll be a real scorcher this week, folks. Keep those animals indoors. Hydrate, hydrate, hydrate.* None of the screens are slashed, and everything is in its right place. Ana's textbooks, Clifton's old bike, the Edward Curtis prints fixed to the fridge, the sterling and turquoise jewelry from Mom hidden inside the closet. There's also a stack of bills on the nightstand. Rent money. Not half like Clifton usually pays. All of it. Ana runs

. . . . . . . .

her hands along the empty bed. A drowning sense of dread hits her face like dirt, slowly until she feels buried. She tries his number twice, the phone dead each time. Maybe the money wasn't from Clifton. Maybe it was Mom. Who knows? Ana does know one thing. She'd rather not sleep alone tonight.

"Goddamn you," Ana whispers and packs a bag for Mom's.


The house is silent apart from buzzing appliances and the muted drafts of Mom's snores. She lives in the suburbs in a ranch-style home off Wadsworth Boulevard. A decade ago, she sold her bungalow on the Northside to a young attorney couple from Philadelphia. They immediately painted the yellow house gray, marking it unrecognizable to anyone from the past. Didn't Louisa Garcia once live here? Wasn't this block the Hispanic or Italian side of town? No one asks questions like this anymore. No one remembers and no one cares.

In the guest bedroom, Ana strips, dropping her clothes where she stands. She slides into the bed with its brass frame originally from her grandparents. Ana holds the brass for a long moment, her palms picking up a metallic scent like blood. She then moves her hands along her sweat-slicked body, neck to thighs. Years ago, in this bed, Clifton reached behind Ana's back, tossing aside her long hair as he fumbled with bra straps. Mom was at work. The bedroom door was open. Ana was sixteen, newly in love. She folded her arms, revealing, as if suddenly, her full-moon breasts. With a hungry mouth, Clifton kissed her cusps and held her tightly in each hand.

*You make me feel full,* he told her more than once. *I'm heavy with you.*

———

· · · · · · ·

"Morning." Ana kisses Mom's cheek as she stands before the kitchen sink, peering out the window at the brittle lawn. A crystal prism dangles, rainbowless and still.

"There's oatmeal in the pantry." Mom's dark eyes search the backyard. A blue jay dives from the sky, bumping against a waterless birdbath, knocking its beak into cement before fluttering away.

"They say it's supposed to get even hotter this week." Ana grabs a banana and takes a seat at the table.

"Who says that?"

"The weather people. They say it's the worst drought in four hundred years."

Mom turns away from the window. She sits at the table with perfect posture, carrying her weight like armor, wearing a string of Bisbee turquoise, lying just so across her breasts. "All you're having is a banana? You'll disappear, jita. Have some eggs. I'll fry them for you."

Ana lets her mother cook for her. She watches as Mom removes the carton of brown eggs from the fridge, cracking them lightly into a white bowl. As she whisks, Mom's hands curve along her thumbs, meeting wide, capable palms. Ana loves her mother's hands, their road map lines and graceful nails.

"Why aren't you at your apartment?" Mom looks over her shoulder. "Did you miss my cooking?"

Ana considers telling Mom the truth, that Clifton is gone again. That this time is longer than ever before. But Mom can be kinder than Ana and more perceptive. She'll call in to work, searching the worst motels, the darkest bars, anywhere she can think of. All the places Clifton tends to hide. "I was hungry and I have no groceries. And it's really hot, and I have no air-conditioning."

"Or," says Mom, "perhaps you're stressed about some silly

class. You must have inherited your memory from a white man."
She laughs, and laughs again. "Oh, that's right. You did."

Mom often jokes about Ana's long-gone dad, a white guy
from Texas, the one who left before she was born, the man who
had said to *get rid of it, if you're smart.*

Mom serves Ana a plate of fried eggs with two corn tortillas.
She then reaches above the hutch where she keeps her nursing
diploma and framed pictures of Ana. She pulls down a cedar
box, opens it to reveal a beaded purse.

"Do you remember your great-grandfather Desiderio?"

Ana remembers a few fragments of Great-Grandpa Desi. The
fuzzy way her face reflected in his glasses, his warm skin, waxy
and cracked, the fragrance of his tobacco and Old Spice, the
lullaby sounds of his languages, Spanish and something else.
"He died when I was so little, Mom."

"It doesn't have to be a story-memory," she says. "It can be
a picture, a feeling." Mom is seated sideways in her chair, her
abundant form curved outward. She wears her lilac scrubs, her
hair braided with a matching purple ribbon to show solidarity
for one cause or another, maybe war veterans or victims of mass
shootings. "This was his. It carried tobacco for ceremony."

Ana lifts the old-fashioned purse from the table, surprised by
its weightiness.

"You know," Mom says, "Clifton once told me this purse
depicts the emergence, the place where our people crawled out
of the earth. It's down south, near the San Juan Mountains."

Ana examines the purse. It has four mountains in white,
blue, yellow, and black. She rubs her fingers over the center. A
row of beads loosens.

"You come from this land, jita. Remembering that might
help with your little history class."

—

"Ghost sickness," says Brown, "is a culture-bound syndrome of the Navajo and other southwestern tribes." She speaks with pink gum in her tight mouth. "Taken out of its cultural context, the illness doesn't exist."

Ana takes notes in blue ink, only occasionally drifting to the notebook's margin to draw spirals and little eyeballs with long lashes. *Imaginary illness,* she writes, *comes after abrupt/violent death of loved one. Marked by loss of appetite, sense of fear, xtrme cases, hallucinations.*

"If one were to go to the doctor today with these symptoms, you'd have what's known as anxiety or depression. Modern medicine handles it without all-night dances and prayer ceremonies," says Brown sarcastically.

Colleen raises her hand. "Will this be on the final?"

Brown scratches her left eyebrow, smearing her pen's ink across her cheek. "No, Colleen," she says, "but as extra credit, I often ask a question related to Native Americans."

Ana scribbles down the words *extra credit*. She keeps her pen moving, as if memory were dependent upon constant motion. The study guide on her desk reads more like a contract than a learning supplement. What happened at Sand Creek? What land did Juan de Ulibarrí claim for Spain? What caused the Pueblo Revolt of 1680? Ana knows these things. She swears it. With the revolt, the Spanish burned the masks, the prayer sticks, the beaded purses. There is something about every man in the pueblos having his right foot sawed off. There is an image of wet blood dripping from meat and bone into dry sand. There are prayer songs lost forever in the gutted throats of the massacred. Ana raises her hand, surprising even herself.

"Yes," Brown says, searching her class list. "Erica, you have a question?"

"Ana. I'm Ana Garcia."

Brown apologizes. She asks Ana to continue.

"The Pueblo Revolt of 1680, wasn't there a drought then, too?"

Brown is silent as she looks downward, rotating her watchband. "Ana, it'd be wise to follow along. I'm essentially giving you the answers, and right now we're discussing the Land Act of 1820."

Ana murmurs an apology. She tips her gaze toward her lap.

For the remainder of class, Brown lectures, answers appropriate questions, and shakes her head, *no, not quite,* when a front-row student compares the cliff dwellings of Mesa Verde to the grandeur of Notre Dame.


Ana sits before the television on her hardwood floor, her history textbook open between her sticky legs. On the news, there is talk of brush fires and an elderly man found dead on his sofa. Heat exhaustion, the newspeople say. No one noticed he hadn't left the place in days, but the stench, the neighbor woman complained, was awfully ripe, like the smell of a deer crushing against her headlights four years earlier. Ana nervously bites the insides of her cheeks until she tastes blood. She attempts to study while the room turns from day to night. The walls glow violet. The floor disengages into gray. Ana paces in the dark, calling Clifton repeatedly, losing track of time. An empty feeling grows inside her until she decides to turn it off.

The bathwater steams, blurring the mirror above the sink. Ana wipes through the distortion. She has carried candles from her bedroom, one vanilla and the other of St. Michael, placing them at the corners of the tub. The water is rose-colored beneath pink-tiled walls. All summer Ana has avoided baths and their heat, but tonight she eases into the tub, submerging her face as long as her lungs can stand. Beneath the water, Ana hears far-off dings and ticks. She hears the scraping of sand, the pull of soil. From above, she imagines she is small, her dark hair widening in inky tendrils.

That's when she sees Clifton. He is driving the narrow mountain pass between Silverton and Ouray, the Million Dollar Highway, a road once thought impossible to build, the cliffs too steep, the land forsaken. It's deep into the night. The pavement is bone dry as Clifton tilts left then right along the corkscrew path. He is going very fast in a Ford pickup, a cyclops with one headlight. The truck hugs several bends in the road. A black bear, dopey and confused, emerges from the shadowed tree line. Clifton swerves, the drop into the gulch unmeasurable in real time. Thousands of feet the tiny pickup plunges. Thousands of feet Clifton tumbles into the canyon below, into the beginning world of darkness. The pickup resembles a falling star as it sinks into the earth.

In a violent rush, Ana forces herself up from beneath the water's wall. Her left hand is tilted over the tub's brim, her wrist and fingers leaking onto the white and black checkered floor. She gasps, the sound of her lungs echoing throughout the candlelit bathroom. For several moments, her tender chest swells with damp air. She begins to cry.

Ana knows—as certain as she is alive— that Clifton is dead. She allows this sense to search wider, a feeling so vast it could move above cities, across prairies, along granite rocks, plunging headlong into the cool ground. With her left foot, Ana knocks loose the rubber plug, leaning back as the water flows forward.

"I'm scared," she says later, calling Mom. "I think Clifton's gone."

———

"I don't want to see anything," says Brown. "Only the test and your pencils. No cellphones. No extra paper." She writes the exam's start and end times on the green chalkboard. She has advised students to return their completed tests, facedown, on her podium by forty-five after. Brown walks the aisles in modest clog sandals, laying finals, one by one, across each desk. "I wish you the best of luck, and I hope your studying pays off." Brown strolls toward the back windows. Ana glances outside one last time at the dead grass, the expanse of birch trees. There is a sound like falling ice as dusty blinds cover the classroom windows.

The test is what Ana expects—multiple choice for hundreds of questions. A, B, C, or D. Nothing more. Nothing less. The cast of characters is lengthy and time is vacant. What year was the Homestead Act? Which religious group settled the West to avoid persecution? Who became known as Boy General? Ana watches the backs of her classmates' heads, dreams of their answers, their clarity of thought. She finds herself tapping her pencil over letters, guessing far too many times. She shakes her legs. She ties and unties her hair, sweeps fallen strands from her desk onto the carpeted floor. Soon students rise from their seats, turning their tests in to Brown with triumphant looks. Ana remains. She continues to guess. Colleen rises from her chair, heading to the front of the classroom, her blond head held high as a warhorse's. She whispers a thank-you to Brown and exits the classroom, once and for all.

When Ana tallies the number of answers she is certain are correct, the outcome isn't good. A dismal fifteen or twenty, another failing grade. And just when Ana throws her head down in a type of shame, she flips to the last page. Extra credit.

*For a full letter grade increase, in detail, describe the origin myth of the Navajo people.*

Clifton once held Ana's hair high above her neck. Front to back they stood in the chilly light of their apartment bathroom, one week after moving in. Ana loved being with Clifton in their apartment. She loved him holding her body to his in that small white space.

"Calm down, baby," he said. Ana couldn't stop crying, tears and snot streaming down her face in shiny pathways. With her eyes scrunched and her mouth twisted tight, Clifton laughed. All this, he told her, over a tick. "Where did you feel it, again?"

"Right there. Where your hand is." Ana forced Clifton's left hand to the back of her right ear. She held him there, frantic and moaning. That morning had been good. They'd hiked Eldorado Canyon, awake with the first light of dawn. The aspen trees had turned, their golden leaves shimmering. Air felt virtuous to breathe, running through them as thrilling as their pulse, generating its own warmth, its own beat. They laughed and chased one another through narrow granite squeezes, running their palms along cold wet rocks. They eventually slipped into the empty cavity of an old Forest Service shed, where they made love quickly and halfway clothed.

"See it!" There, Clifton explained, tucked into the soft scoop behind Ana's right earlobe was the tick. "This little bastard thinks he's gonna suck my woman? Disrespectful as hell."

Ana bent forward. "Stop laughing. Get it off me. They cause Lyme."

"Grab your hair while I get a match."

She reached up with both hands, taking her hair from Clifton as he rummaged through the drawers, revealing a yellow pack of liquor store matches. He lit one and burned the needle. Clifton went toward Ana with the red tip.

"You have to stand still," he said. "If not, I'll miss the head."

Ana's legs trembled. She asked what happens then.

"Nothing good. They can regrow a body inside you, in your heart." Clifton laughed. "Sorry, babe."

Ana hyperventilated, shaking so much that removal was impossible.

Clifton pleaded with her to calm down. He said it'd be quick. He told her to listen. "How about a story?"

Ana said flatly, "A story? What?"

"You can pay attention to something else." Clifton kissed Ana's shoulder, slick with fear. "Okay—so that buddy of mine Taylor and I were at McNard's dive on Federal when this dude came in selling stolen TVs—"

"A bar story?" Ana did laugh, but only a little.

"Well, excuse me. What do you want? A thriller? Oh, a ghost story."

"No," said Ana. "Tell me something nice."

Clifton was quiet for some time and Ana knew he had stories, some from Mom, some from his own life, some he couldn't quite shake. He said at last, wonderful and low, "How about a Diné story, the beginning of it all."

"Go on," said Ana, her legs slowing to a shudder.

"You have to pay attention. The story has twists. Only in the end is there love."

And so Clifton told Ana the story of First Man and First Woman, how they were born of stardust and earth, scrambled out of the underground land of darkness and traveled through many worlds, leaving behind the blackness of their beginnings for a life of sunlight and air. Clifton removed the tick while Ana, soundless and peaceful, listened in such a way that she knew she'd remember every word for all her life.

"And that," he said when they were finished, "is our story of everything."

# ACKNOWLEDGMENTS

. . . . . . . . . . . . . . . . .

To begin, I thank my ancestors who started their work as artists and storytellers generations before I was born. This book may have taken a decade to write, but its path was set in motion by the undying spirit of my people who have resided in the Southwest since the beginning of this time. Our stories are not forgotten.

To my exceedingly brilliant editor, Nicole Counts. Thank you for trusting my vision, for ushering my work into the world, and for changing my life. To everyone at One World—Chris Jackson, Victory Matsui, and Cecil Flores. What a gift of chance that my work ended up at this groundbreaking imprint. Thank you for the books you're bringing to our world.

To my agent, my friend, Julia Masnik. My deepest gratitude to you for taking me on, pushing my abilities, protecting my work, and guiding me on this journey. Here's to our first book together.

Thank you to the residencies that gave me space and nourishment: MacDowell Colony, the Corporation of Yaddo, and Hedgebrook. And to my MFA program at the University of Wyoming, where I was given two years to develop a thesis that would later become *S&C*. To the writers who encouraged me and kept me from giving up—Ann Beattie, Junot Diaz, Alyson Hagy, Mat Johnson, Rattawut Lapcharoensap, Beth Loffreda, Daniel Menaker, Stephen-Paul Martin, Brad Watson, and Joy Williams. And thank you to Michael and Kathy Blades for helping me and my writing when I needed it most.

To my community in Denver—What up, Mile High City! Lighthouse Writers, the Chicana/o Studies Department at MSUD, and the whole West Side Books crew, especially Lois Harvey, my second mother, this one adorned in books.

To my friends who have become family. Ivelisse Rodriguez, thank you for your work and for our many years as writing sisters. I am grateful to Sebastian Doherty, who made life as a writer seem possible. Thank you to Trent Segura for his genius research and exquisite taste. Thank you to Lauren Treihaft, Jamie McKinney, and Joey Rubin, who read drafts of these stories and offered their guidance. And thank you to Lauren Clabaugh, who housed me in Tucson while I wrote the first draft of "Sisters" one blazing summer.

And most of all, my enormous Wild West family. Thank you to my mother, Renee Fajardo, for her unruliness, beauty, and for the deep sense of justice she instilled in her seven children. To my father, Glen Anstine, for delivering books to my door when I was a depressed teenager. Papa, you always had faith in my abilities as an artist. To my six siblings—Asia, Avalon, Sydney, Tim, Dylan, and Piper—what a world we shared growing up, and what best friends I have found in you as adults. To my grandparents, and to my godmother, Joanna Lucero, for gifting me with their stories. To my partner, Tyler, for teaching me that we are all deserving of great love.

And to the girls—may you see yourselves in books, may you write your own, and may your strength burn brighter than any sun.

# Sabrina & Corina

# &

# Corina

Kali Fajardo-Anstine

A READER'S GUIDE

# QUESTIONS AND TOPICS FOR DISCUSSION

· · · · · · · · · · · · · · · · ·

1. Did this book teach you something new about the American West? If so, what?

2. Many of the protagonists in *Sabrina & Corina* are presented with a type of twinning character. Which characters seemed to complement each other, for better or worse?

3. What is the importance of storytelling in *Sabrina & Corina*? In what ways do the characters tell one another stories, and for what reasons?

4. Fajardo-Anstine presents her female characters as pillars of strength and women with flaws. Why do you think the author did this?

5. What did *Sabrina & Corina* teach you about the Latinx and indigenous experiences in the United States?

6. Many of the characters in *Sabrina & Corina* are ethnically mixed. How does the author highlight these hybrid identities?

7. A sense of home and one of place and are very important in *Sabrina & Corina*. How do the different characters in these stories define home, as well as their place in society and among their families? And how do you as a reader define the concept of home?

8. Why do you think Fajardo-Anstine explored violence against women in this community?

9. Fajardo-Anstine has said that she wrote *Sabrina & Corina* out of a need to understand why beauty and death were linked so closely in her culture. How do you see those elements in these stories?

10. Many of the stories in *Sabrina & Corina* are set in the fictional town of Saguarita. What other memorable fictional towns have you encountered in literature?

QUESTIONS SPECIFIC TO STORIES:

. . . . . . . . . . . . . . . . . . .

1. What does Sierra's sugar "baby" represent to you?

2. What do you think happened to Lucia Barrera in "Sisters"?

3. How has gentrification impacted characters in stories like "Galapago" and "Tomi"?

4. In "Any Further West," do you think Neva will break the cycle of violence in her family?

5. Education plays an important role in "Ghost Sickness." How does that story challenge dominant narratives about the American West?

KALI FAJARDO-ANSTINE is from Denver, Colorado. She is the author of *Sabrina & Corina*, a finalist for the National Book Award, the PEN/Robert W. Bingham Prize, the LaVerne Harrell Clark Fiction Prize, The Story Prize, the Saroyan Prize, and winner of an American Book Award. She is also the 2021 recipient of the Addison M. Metcalf Award from the American Academy of Arts and Letters. Her work has been honored with the Denver Mayor's Global Award for Excellence in Arts & Culture, and the Mountains and Plains Independent Booksellers Association Reading the West Book Award for Fiction. She has written for *The New York Times, Harper's Bazaar, ELLE, Oprah Daily, The American Scholar, Boston Review,* and elsewhere, and has received fellowships from MacDowell, Yaddo, Hedgebrook, and Tin House. Fajardo-Anstine earned her MFA from the University of Wyoming and has lived across the country, from Durango, Colorado, to Key West, Florida. She is the 2022–2023 Endowed Chair in Creative Writing at Texas State University.

kalifajardoanstine.com
Twitter: @KaliMaFaja
Instagram: @kalimaja

To inquire about booking Kali Fajardo-Anstine for a speaking engagement, please contact the Penguin Random House Speakers Bureau at speakers@penguinrandomhouse.com.